The Dance

My First Love

Kristy Cato

I dedicate this book

To my first love, my one and only true love,

JEANNA B.

THANK YOU FOR THE DANCE

AND FOR THE WONDERFUL YEARS.

YOU TAUGHT ME ALOT, I WILL ALWAYS LOVE YOU.

Author's Note

When I was growing up, there were no books out there like this to tell everyone it's okay to love who you love. So I write what's in my heart, hoping people will like it and, more importantly, relate to it. I wanted to write about love that is never expressed this way, in a loving way.

Please join me in these stories.

Content

Chapter One: On My

Own. . . . .

. . . .1

Chapter Two: A New

World. . . . .

. . . .5

Chapter Three: Wow: What Are These Feelings? 7

Chapter Four: The Plans We Made 2 5

Chapter Five: The College

Years . . . .

. 29

Chapter Six: Something Just Doesn't Feel

Right . . . .

. 33

Chapter Seven: New Friends Aren't

Always Good

Friends. . . . .

. 45

Chapter Eight: She's Back and Things

Aren't Always as They

Seem. . . . .

. 61

Chapter Nine: Whoever Said You Can

Go Home Again

Lied..

..............................70

Chapter Ten: I Will Never Be the

Same.....................................

.............................77

Chapter Eleven: The Dance Is

Over.....................................

.............................84

Chapter Twelve: I Never Knew It Could Be Like This While I'm Missing You..100

Chapter Thirteen: Under the Same Roof..113

Chapter Fourteen: A Familiar Town but Things Are Not the

Same............................

...........................131

Chapter Fifteen: Good-bye, My

Love...

...............156

Chapter One

On My Own

Imagine being six years old standing on a stage, looking out toward a room full of parents gathered to celebrate the first of what will likely be just one of many achievements, a child's first graduation. Kindergarten in California is an exciting time, not just for kids who get to wear white robes and receive little awards to signify they're moving on to the first grade, but also for parents, some of whom bring flowers as they arrive and some who come with neatly wrapped gifts of celebration in honor of this special day. It can also be a sad day, especially for one little girl who woke up on this special day knowing that before she left for school, her mother wasn't home nor was she anywhere to be found. That was me, Carrie.

Looking back now, I wonder how I was able to get myself up, make myself a bowl of cereal, take a shower, brush my sandy brown shoulder-length hair, and head off to school to my graduation. I was young and very used to taking care of myself. My mother was either drunk or hardly ever around. As most young girls are, I was a sweet girl who needed to be loved, and I continually looked for it from my mother but couldn't seem to ever get it. It became easy to be quiet and reserved, because I didn't have much interaction with other kids. I was petite, and as I was often told, I had the prettiest walnut-brown eyes and always kept a smile on my face. I can recall hanging on to hope inside that one day my own mother would see this in me, and that one day she would love me.

I did well in school, kept my room clean, and stayed out of her way, as a way of trying to make her happy. I loved my mother and this was the only way I knew how to show her that. Most importantly, I wanted to spend time with her.

I recall getting to school that day. Tables were being set up in the room for everyone attending. On top of each table were names of the kids' parents. All of us kids were asked to stand in line and give our family's names and the number of chairs we would need for our family members. My teacher noticed that I wasn't in line. When she finished with all the other kids, she walked over to me and said that I needed to give her my family count and their names so my table could be set up. I looked up at my blonde teacher, whose shoes were slightly worn and whose dress I remember having static cling at the bottom. She stood only about five feet two inches tall.

"My mom is my only family member and she can't make it," I said.

She was kind to me and said, "Well then, you can sit with the teachers until it's time to go on stage."

I felt nervous, but I said, "Okay, thank you."

While all the teachers gave their speeches and served us punch and cookies, I looked around the room at all the kids having a good time with their families, and wished it were me. After graduation was over, I walked home. I was a latch-key kid, so when I arrived home, I let myself in.

I arrived home to find that my mom still wasn't home. I don't even think she came home the night before. She did that a lot, which meant most of the time, I was on my own. I sat down to watch TV, hoping my mom would be home soon to make some dinner, but by 8 p.m. when she still wasn't home, I decided to make myself a peanut butter sandwich. I had to scrape the mold off of the bread because mom hadn't gone food shopping in a while. There was nothing to eat, really, other than cereal, a jar with barely any peanut butter left in it, and a little bit of milk, which I was saving for my cereal in the morning.

Growing up, I didn't really have a bedtime because Mom was hardly ever home. When she was, she would just send me to bed when one of her boyfriends was with her, or when she just didn't want to be bothered with me. Although my mom would go through boyfriends what seemed like every month, they were always the center of her attention.

That night, I fell asleep watching TV. It was around 1:30 a.m. when my mom arrived home drunk, yelling at me to turn off the TV and go to bed. Sometimes I stayed in the living room with the TV on because I was afraid to be in the house by myself, which happened often.

The next morning Mom was home. I tried to show her my graduation certificate, but she barely glanced at it before putting it down on the table. There was no "I'm proud of you" and no "I'm sorry I couldn't make it." Later on that day, I found my graduation certificate under a glass with water rings on it, as if she had been using it for a coaster. I took it, wiped it dry, and put it away.

My mom was a big drinker, which made her look a lot older than she actually was. I didn't know how old my mother was at that time, but I remember her looking really old to me. She could be pretty scary at times, with her dark black hair and bags under what I assumed used to be her pretty blue eyes. She usually looked so worn out and beaten up—scary, like I said—which for a little girl is not what you want to see. I spent plenty of time playing in my room by myself and did lots of reading, because I wasn't allowed to have friends over. I wished so badly that I had a brother or sister. I felt really lonely playing on my own all of the time.

By the time I was eight, it became clear to me that my mother hated me, yet I didn't know why. I remember her saying mean things to condemn me and she put me down all of the time. She told me I was a waste of time and space. I just tried to stay out of her way. I knew to never ask for anything because she always said she didn't have any money. When I was ten, one of the girls in my class passed out invitations to her eleventh birthday party. I couldn't believe I was invited to my first birthday party. I had never been to one, let alone had one of my own. I was so excited when I got home! I showed my mother the invitation and asked if I could go. She said, "Sure."

I ran to my bedroom to find my best dress, though I knew I didn't have many.

The dress I picked out was a pretty pink one that was bought at the thrift shop, like all the rest of

my clothes. I asked my mom if we could go out and buy a present.

"If you have to bring something to the party, then you can't go," she said.

I told her I didn't have to bring anything, just so I could go. I knew I wanted to bring something, so instead of buying a gift, I got some paper and a handful of markers and made what I thought was a really pretty card. I was so proud of it, I couldn't wait until Saturday!

On Friday, I double-checked with my mom to make sure she was still going to take me to the party; she assured me that she was. Although the party wasn't until 3 p.m., on Saturday morning I awoke really early, full of excitement about going to the party. I went into the kitchen to make myself a bowl of cereal and noticed Mom wasn't home. I ate, I watched cartoons, and waited for time to pass, hoping for my mother to come home. Around 1:30 p.m. I got tired of waiting, so I decided I would get dressed for the party. I grabbed my card off my dresser and sat on the couch, waiting patiently for my mother to come home. At 2:30 p.m. I started to get nervous. I had a sick feeling and somehow knew she wasn't coming home.

Needless to say, I woke up on the couch later that night around. I got up off the couch, went into my room, took off my dress, and got in bed, crying myself to sleep. I was no longer afraid to sleep in the house alone from that night on, because I realized no one would ever hurt me as much as my mom did. After that night, I never asked her for anything ever again.

Chapter Two

A New World

By the time I was fifteen, I was really good at staying out of my mother's way and doing my own thing, which meant keeping to myself. Sometimes I got to come home and sometimes I didn't; it usually depended on if she needed me to stay away because her boyfriends were at our house. Since I had no friends, I learned to be creative about where I would stay for the night. Aside from that, all I ever did was homework and listen to music in my room on the clock radio. I also read a lot. I promised myself that when I had kids, I would spend lots of time with them and give them all the love I always wanted but never got from my own mom. I knew I wanted at least two kids. Being an only child was very lonely and I didn't ever want them to feel the loneliness that I did growing up. I knew the kind of mom I wanted to be. I wanted to give them all the birthday parties I never got to have and I wanted every Christmas we would someday share together to be the best that any kid would ever dream of having. I planned to take them to all the places my mother never took me, like the zoo and the circus. I know it seems like I should have gone to some of these places on school field trips, but it cost money to go with your class and my mom never had any. Well, at least that's what she told me.

I was always that kid who had to stay behind in the library while my class was away. One time, I was left behind and felt so happy to find a book that told all about the circus. I was having so much fun reading this book, even as I saw all of my classmates arriving back from the field trip that day with popcorn, balloons, and hats. I wasn't sure what to think. I didn't feel sorry for myself, though, because sadly, I didn't know any different. I thought this was the way it was supposed to be and that I could do all of these things with my kids when I grew up. I learned to focus on my future as a way of distracting myself from the life I was in. I knew I was going to get a great job so that one day, I would have the money to take my kids places and see everything we wanted together, for the first time. It gave me hope, something to look forward to.

When I got to high school, I wanted to make friends. I remember thinking, though, what was the point if I could never have them over? I did manage to meet a few boys, but I never really had a boyfriend. As most teenage girls do, I kissed a few boys, but nothing serious ever came of it. I just really wasn't into it. My plan was to get a scholarship to college, live in the dorms, and make lots of friends. All I had to do was keep my grades up and get through the next two years. Then I would be free to go and be happy.

Chapter Three

Wow: What Are These

Feelings?

I was about sixteen years old when I realized I was attracted to females. It was a typical day; I had just come from my gym class when I entered the locker room to take a shower. While undressing, I noticed a girl sitting on a bench in front of the lockers. I had never seen her before. She had dark black hair and smooth olive skin. She had the looks of an actress and if she'd been a little taller, she could have been a model. She was slim, had beautiful blue eyes, and full lips. She looked up at me and smiled, so I smiled back and said "Hi, I'm Carrie." She said she was a new student and that her name was Kim. She had just moved here from Arizona. We made small talk, and I asked how she liked L.A.

"It seems to be okay, so far," she said, "but it's a little different from Arizona. I guess I'll have to get used to it since I have to live here now."

Kim was that kind of girl that was cute and pretty. You know, pretty and cute at the same time. She had a beautiful smile along with her pretty blue eyes. I just smiled at her and said, "I guess I better get into the shower; I don't want to be late to my next class."

Kim smiled. "Yeah, I'm jumping in there in a minute."

As I entered the shower, I could not get her smile out of my mind. I noticed when she entered the shower that she had a heart tattooed on her left arm with the initials C.J. I wondered who C.J. was and how Kim had been able to get a tattoo at such a young age.

As I headed to my next class, I could not get Kim out of my head. I knew she was going to be my new friend. But then I thought no, because it would not be a good idea to have a friend, knowing I couldn't bring her home with me. Maybe she would just be someone I would have small talk with after gym class. At lunchtime, I went to find my favorite tree to sit under, where I like to eat and listen to music while at Encino High. Encino High School is full of famous actors and actress kids, some trying to follow in their parents' footsteps, some becoming snobs, and some trying to change the world. Then you had your punk rockers, hippies, et cetera. I never really made an effort to make friends at school. God forbid if I brought one home; my mother didn't really want me there, let alone one of my friends. But now, I had met Kim.

Sitting under the tree that day, I was about to take a bite of my sandwich when I felt someone tap me on the shoulder. I looked up to see it was Kim and her pretty smile looking down at me.

"Hey," she said. "Can I join you, or is this tree only reserved for you?"

I smiled back. "No, please, join me."

She sat down and we talked about her old school in comparison to this school and why she moved here. It turned out she was actually born here in Los Angeles. Her mother was an actress who had been in a sitcom some years back. Kim's mom was trying to get back into show business, so they moved back to Los Angeles to try her luck again. Kim was really down to earth; she didn't seem shallow like lots of the kids here. For the next two weeks, we ate lunch under my favorite tree every day. We loved the same type of movies and music. It seemed like we could talk for hours. Sometimes we did and found ourselves late for class.

One Friday afternoon, while eating lunch, Kim asked what I would be doing for the weekend.

"Not much," I said. "Just hanging out and listening to music."

"Why don't you come over for the weekend? My mom is going to New York and I hate to be alone."

I told her I would check with my mom, knowing that my mom would love to get me out of the house. That Friday evening, my mom dropped me off on her way to her boyfriend's house. We pulled up at a big house on the corner of Bob Hope Drive. I had no idea Kim lived in such a big beautiful house. Even my mom said, "Wow!" as I exited the car.

Kim came running out to meet me with a big hug. I had no idea we had moved on to affection, but I can tell you, I had never felt a hug that I wanted so bad. I introduced Kim to my mother, and as my mother drove away, I knew I was in trouble. I had no idea what was happening to me, or my body. All I knew was that I was feeling something that I had never felt before. Everything was new to me.

I was sixteen and still a virgin. Sure, I had kissed boys before but never really felt anything. There is a feeling you get, a tingling inside your stomach that I was just discovering. This excited me and also made me nervous. All I knew was that I had to watch myself and I knew that spending the whole weekend alone with her was going to be hard. I loved being around Kim; she was always so sweet. As I entered her house and stood there in her very large foyer, I was blown away. While I was looking around, I noticed a large picture of a very pretty woman. I asked who it was. She said it was her mother who she hardly got to spend time with lately even though they were very close. When I looked at the picture again, I realized it was the famous actress April Springs. I had no idea. I mean, Kim said her mother used to be an actress, but I guess I never figured it was April Springs. I used to watch her show all the time! She played the part of a teenager who was always getting in trouble on a sitcom, back before I was even born. I used to love watching the reruns. I had also seen her in a few movies, and now here I was in her house!

I was very careful to not touch anything. As we walked through the living room we passed all kinds of family pictures, many of Kim as a little girl, yet no sign of her father around.

I understood since my father wasn't in my life. My mother once told me my father had left her before I was born, which made me wonder if he even knew I existed. I still yearned for the day my mother would tell me she loved me, but so far it had not happened. Hearing Kim talk about her and her mother being so close got me thinking about the one time I told my mother I loved her, hoping she would say it back to me. She was dropping me off at school, which she didn't do very often. It was raining and I had a project I needed to turn in. I didn't want it to get wet, so after begging her to drop me off at school, I opened the door to get out of the car. I thanked her and said, "I love you, Mom," but she yelled to close the door and said, "You're letting the rain in!" and then drove off. Because the rain was pouring down on me, no one could see I had tears rolling down my face. I knew she would never love me.

Kim's house was so beautiful and I really was afraid to touch anything. We headed for the kitchen where she had a bunch of snacks laid out for us. She also had movies out for us to watch. All the movies were classics—my favorite, *Imitation of Life*, along with *A Place in the Sun*. I couldn't even say how many times I'd seen that movie; I just loved Elizabeth Taylor. And there was another one I'd never heard of called *The Children's Hour*.

Imitation of Life is a very long movie, which took up most of the night. We fell asleep in front of the TV, and when I woke up in the morning, I smelled breakfast cooking. It was a nice change from my house. It seemed like I had to pray every morning, hoping for cereal to eat. When I went into the kitchen, a short round woman was cooking. I walked in looking for Kim and said, "Hello, I'm Carrie."

The woman looked at me and said, "Yes, you're Kim's friend. She should be out of the shower soon. I'm Rosa, the maid and cook. Are you hungry?"

"Yes ma'am, thank you."

She smiled and said, "Have a seat at the table and it will be right over."

While sitting there, all I could think about was last night during the movie. I was wondering if Kim ever noticed how many times I looked over at her pretty face and if she suspected anything about how

I felt about her. As Kim entered the kitchen she said, "Good morning, sleepy head."

I came out of my daze and said, "Good morning" back to her.

"Are you ready to eat?" she said. "Rosa is my favorite cook! You'll love her food. Rosa cooks for me whenever Mom's out of town."

"Does your mom cook for you?" I asked.

"All the time," Kim answered.

"When does she have time, doesn't she have to work and go to meetings?"

"Yes, but my mom puts me before all of that." I just looked at her, thinking as busy as her mom gets, her mother still had time for her. It must have been obvious I was sad as I sat there, not being able to remember one single day that my mom put me before anything, because Kim asked me, "Are you okay?"

I paused and said, "Yes," acknowledging her and trying to enjoy eating breakfast with her.

That afternoon, we headed to the mall in Kim's car. I thought it was cool that she had her own car. We basically window shopped as we talked and laughed the afternoon away. It was like there was no one else there but us. I couldn't seem to get enough of Kim. She also had this uncanny way of touching my hand. Every time she touched me, I got this tingling feeling inside of me. She took me to the movies, and during the whole movie, she held my hand. At one point, she put her head on my shoulder. We went back to her house that night and fell asleep while watching *A Place in the Sun*.

The next morning, my mother picked me up early. I spent the entire afternoon daydreaming about Kim in my room, as I listened to music while trying to get my homework done.

Kim and I hung out all the time after that. I would spend the night over her house a lot. As time went by, we got to know each other a lot better. I was falling in love with her. When she found out I didn't have money like she did, she would take me to the movies, out to lunch, and to different places. I really didn't care where we went; I just wanted to be with her. She had no idea that she was taking me places I had never been before, even somewhere as simple as a restaurant. My mom never took me anywhere, so this was all new to me. It wasn't as if I didn't know about all these different places, because I would see them and read about them in books. I was a big reader; it was the only way I got to experience things before I met Kim. The only place my mom ever took me was a thrift shop for school clothes, which was exciting to me. And I got to wait in the car once while she went into the bar where she worked to pick up her paycheck. I think I was six at the time.

I was having so much fun with Kim and really enjoyed seeing things and places that I had read about so many times. I felt so happy. It wasn't until one day at school when I was walking down the hall to my locker and saw Kim talking to a boy named Mike that I got upset. Mike was known at our school as the big football star. Everybody knew he was a ladies' man, but he was so charming. Even after he would dump a girl, everyone still loved him and only had good things to say about him. To see them standing there talking made my heart drop! I could no longer feel anything. I suddenly went numb. I couldn't comprehend what she was doing, or why she was talking to the guy known for sleeping with girls and then dumping them. I walked to my locker, got my books, and then headed to my first class. I ignored Kim when I heard her call my name as I entered the classroom. I was so hurt, but I couldn't let her know, so I tried avoiding her. My plan was to act like I didn't hear her once she caught up to me later. I didn't eat at my favorite tree that day, knowing Kim would or should have met me there. I hid out in the library. I also skipped gym class. If I didn't, I would run into her there and didn't know what I would say. Would she be able to tell she was breaking my heart? Would I be busted? All I wanted was her time and now here I was, hiding from her. I didn't want to share her with anyone. I began thinking this was the end for us. My mind was already playing tricks on me.

When I got home, my mother was sitting in the living room with Kim. I was completely surprised and not prepared to see her. Here I thought I had made a clean break, yet as I walked through the door, Kim looked up and said, "Hey, busy bee, I have been looking for you all day."

All I could say was, "Oh yeah, I was really busy today." As I walked back to my room, I could feel her hand trying to hold mine, but I just pulled away.

When we reached my room, she closed the door and asked, "Are you mad at me?"

I said, "No, why would you ask that?"

Kim quickly replied, "Well, let's see, I called your name in the hallway today and you ignored me. Then you didn't show up for gym, the only class we have together. You also didn't meet me under our tree at lunchtime, and now you're acting funny toward me."

I liked the fact that she called it "our tree." "Wow," I said. "That's a lot, Kim. I can see how you would think something is wrong." I covered my tracks by saying, "Let's see. I didn't hear you calling me and my stomach was hurting, so I went to the nurse and lied down. That's why I wasn't in gym class or at the tree for lunch. What did you want?"

"Talk about wow! Do I have to want something? Aren't we friends? Haven't we been hanging out for the last few months? Oh, let me guess, you're sick of me, Carrie. Is that it?"

I tried to stay calm and said, "Kim, it's just been a bad day. I'm sorry. I just need to lie down for a while, then, I'll be fine. I'll call you later." While I was saying this, I was basically pushing her out the door.

After she left, my mom came into my room and said, "I don't want a bunch of people coming over here! Do you understand?"

"Mom, it was just one friend."

She repeated, "Do you understand?"

"Yes ma'am," I replied. As I had always known, I could never have friends over without my mom getting upset. After she left my room, I went back to thinking about Kim. I was now thinking I needed to put some space between us. What if she started to suspect something? There was no way that I wanted her to find out a girl liked her. What would happen if she did? Would she tell her mom? Would her mom tell my mom? That was it! I needed to avoid her like the plague. But how, without her knowing that I was falling in love with her? How do you all of a sudden stop hanging out with someone you have been hanging out with every day for the last few months without hurting her feelings?

I came up with a plan. I pretended to be sick and did not go to school for the next two days. That gave me some relief, knowing I wouldn't have to deal with her for the next four days. The weekend would come on the day I would be feeling better, so all I had to do was come up with a new plan by Monday.

During the weekend, I found myself wondering if she was going on a date with Mike. What would they be doing if she did? And why, after all of the rumors she'd heard about him, would she even go out with him? Was she going to kiss him or fall for his charming lines and sleep with him? Sometimes my mind began to wonder like crazy. I wished it were me going on that date with her, kissing her, or even just holding her hand. I was starting to miss her. But just when I started to get mad at the thought of her and Mike, someone knocked at my bedroom door. It was her!

Kim had a bag in one hand and a movie in the other. I knew my mother wasn't going to be happy with me having Kim over again. I soon learned, though, that Kim had called my mother to see if it was okay to come over. When my mother told her I wasn't feeling well, she told my mom she wanted to bring over soup, orange juice, and a movie. All I could do was smile, because I was so happy to see her, but I was also wondering why wasn't she out with Mike? She came inside and hugged me, then told me she came over to make me feel better. She couldn't deal with school without me.

What happened to Mike? Why wasn't he having lunch with her at school? Didn't she have a date with him this weekend?

The movie she brought over was the one movie we never got around to watching that first weekend I spent with her, *The Children's Hour*. It starred Shirley MacLaine and Audrey Hepburn. I had never seen this movie or even heard of it. Kim went to my mom and got a bowl. While she was gone, I tried to think of a way to ask her why she wasn't out with Mike. When Kim came back, she sat down and poured the soup into the bowl for me.

"Kim," I said, "when you found out I was sick, didn't you make other plans?"

"When I found out you were sick, all I did was make plans to help you feel better."

She was so sweet that way. "So I didn't take you from any other plans you had before you found out I was sick?"

She laughed and said, "No, silly, you know all my plans are with you." I sat there thinking for a few minutes, and then I said, "Can I ask you something, Kim?"

"You can ask me anything your heart desires, Carrie."

"Are there any boys at school you're interested in?"

"Nope, no boys at all," she said.

I persisted with the questioning by asking, "Are you sure, Kim?"

"Yep, I'm sure. Why?"

"Well, I saw you talking to Mike in the hallway last week."

"Who?" She sounded shocked.

"You know, Mike, the football player." I could see she was thinking about it.

"Oh," she said. "You mean that big guy who asked me to give a note to some girl in one of my classes? Now, why would I be interested in some big playboy when I have you to fill my days and weekends?"

All I could do was smile, but I also wondered what she meant by that. Kim put the movie in. I had a portable DVD player that I had won in a writing contest. At first I had no idea what was going on in the movie. But then, I soon caught onto the fact that it was about a woman who was in love with another woman, her best friend. When I realized what the plot was, I blurted out, "Oh, that poor woman!"

Kim smiled, then leaned in and kissed me, dead on my lips.

Oh my God! My heart was pounding so hard, I thought I was going to have a heart attack. Her lips were so soft, like nothing I had ever imagined. This was it; I was in love.

She looked into my eyes and whispered, "Do you have any idea how long I've wanted to do that?"

I effortlessly said, "I love you, Kim." I couldn't hold back any longer. "I've loved you since the first time I saw your smile."

"I love you too, Carrie," she said. "I've loved you since the first weekend you spent at my house."

"Why didn't you tell me, Kim?"

"I did; every time I held your hand, every time I smiled at you, and every time I spent a day with you."

"But you spent every day with me up until Tuesday."

"I know, Carrie. That's how I tried telling you, by showing you. Would you rather me tell you or show you?"

I really wanted her to say it. To say that she loved me, since no one ever had. "Well, what took you so long to kiss me, Kim?"

"I had to wait until I knew it was okay."

"How did you know it was okay to kiss me?"

"By the way you reacted to the movie. Now let's get you better, Carrie."

At that point I sat up cleared my throat and said "Um, Kim, don't be mad at me, please, but I'm not really sick."

She looked at me with surprise and said, "You're not?"

"No, it was more like I was heartbroken. You see, when I saw you talking to Mike in the hallway, I thought you liked him and that you two were getting together. But now that I know the truth about everything, I feel that it's okay to tell you."

"Tell me what?"

"I'm in love with you."

Kim smiled at me. "You're so cute; I love you too!" Then she kissed me again.

"So what do we do now, Kim?"

Kim didn't hesitate when she said, "If you'll have me, Carrie, I would like to be your girlfriend. My mom is going to New York next weekend. You could come over and we could celebrate. What do you think?"

"I think next weekend can't come fast enough." We both laughed.

Kim left my house around 8 p.m. that night. Soon after, my mom came into my room and shouted, "Didn't I tell you I didn't want a bunch of people over here?"

"Yes, but Mom, I never have a bunch of people over; it's just one friend."

"Next time I'm going to put you and your friend out and see where you have to live!" She then slammed my door and left my room. I knew she meant what she was saying, because she had done it several times before. The first time was when I was eight. One of her boyfriends didn't like kids, so she made me find somewhere else to go for the night. I went back to my school and slept in one of the tires they had on the playground. I was so scared, but I didn't have much of a choice. I prayed most of the night, asking God to keep me safe and to let me be able to go home the next day. I told him I was sorry if he was doing this because I was a bad girl and that I would try harder to be good. The next day I waited around the corner and watched until my mother's boyfriend left, and then I knew it was safe to go home. This was something I had to do often.

As the days went by, I started to get more and more excited to be with Kim, but I was worried at the same time. I didn't know what to do and felt nervous because I never had sex before. I began to wonder if she would be okay with it. Did she know what to do? And had she ever had sex before? All I knew was I loved her and I wanted everything to go right.

The bell rang at 3 p.m. on Friday. School was over. I was now going home with my new girlfriend to make love for the very first time. I walked to the front of the school where Kim was waiting for me. Her mom honked her horn to let us know she was there and so we ran to the car, giggling like two little girls. Her mom had dropped her off at school, because whenever she was going out of town, she wanted to see Kim before she left. She said she couldn't go anywhere without a kiss from Kim before leaving.

Her mom dropped us off at their house, gave Kim a kiss good-bye, and said, "Are you going to be okay with me leaving again, Kim?"

Kim said, "Yes, Mom, I have Carrie. She's going to be with me for the whole weekend. Right, Carrie?"

"Yes, I'll stay with you," I replied.

Her mother was clearly happy for her. "Okay," she said. "I love you; be good, girls. I'll be back on Monday."

Kim kissed her mom back and said, "I love you too, Mom. Have a safe flight."

Kim's mom was gorgeous, and she was one of the sweetest women that I had ever met in my life. She had this neat aura about her. And even though she had blue eyes and blond hair, which of course was bleached, you could tell Kim got her looks from her mother. Something about Ms. Springs made me feel welcome in her space.

When we entered Kim's house, I immediately felt nervous. We headed upstairs and dropped off our things in Kim's room.

"Do you want to watch movies and pig out on some junk food?" she asked.

In a really somber tone I said, "Okay, sure."

"Is there something wrong, Carrie?"

I said no when really I wanted to tell her something.

"Come on, Carrie, what's wrong?"

"I can't tell you."

Kim said, "Remember I told you that you can tell me anything."

"It's just that I never, umm . . ."

"You never what?"

I confided in her in a shy voice, "I've never done it before."

Kim looked directly at me and said, "Done what, Carrie?"

So I whispered to her as if someone was around us and said, "You know, it!"

"Oh, you're a virgin and you're worried?"

I shouted, "Yes!"

She smiled and said, "Awe, you don't need to worry," and then she started to laugh.

"It's not funny, Kim."

She giggled. "No, it's not. I just thought something was really wrong, like you didn't want to be here, or that you wanted to go home! You're so cute, Carrie." She leaned in, kissed me, and said, "I promise we won't do anything that you don't want to do; and if you don't want to do anything at all, we don't have to. I just want to be with you, okay?"

So I said, "Okay. But, Kim, I need to know something. Have you ever done it before?"

"Sure." She seems so comfortable talking to me about it.

"But, with a girl?"

"Yes, with a couple of girls and with one boy. That's how I knew I preferred girls over boys."

I was now very curious and asked, "How old were you when you first had sex?"

She was very open and honest with me and said, "I was fifteen."

I kept asking question after question, wanting to know more about her first experience. "Was it with a boy or a girl?"

"It was with a boy, and I didn't like it the first time. It kind of hurt. But the next few times, it didn't hurt much. I just couldn't get into it. Then I met this girl. We had sex and I loved it."

I wondered if that girl was C.J. "How do you know if you're doing it right?" I asked.

"Well, usually, if it feels good to both of you."

I got sort of quiet, trying to imagine what it would feel like. Kim was really great. She was so gentle with me and asked, "Is there anything else you want to know?"

I said, "Nope, not right now."

The first night Kim and I ordered takeout and then ate lots of candy as we watched *If These Walls Could Talk, Part Two.* I thought it was so cool how Kim could just call up and order food. Her mother had set her up so she would never miss a meal, and Kim always made sure I ate. Even when I would go home, she came to my bedroom window and brought food for me. It was cool that she did that for me. She would call me and say, "I made some dinner and I want you to taste it and tell me what you think." I knew she did it because she knew I had either very little or nothing to eat at home. She would bring me so much and say, "Just in case you really like it, I brought you extra." She was always looking out for me; I loved that about her.

After about the third movie, I fell asleep. I was woken up by a kiss. It was the middle of the night and Kim was awake, kissing me all over my neck. She slowly worked her way down to my breast, then back up to my lips. She lowered herself onto me and began to grind on me. She was making me feel so good, there was no turning back and I didn't want her to stop. She began to remove my top, putting her tongue on the tip of my nipple; she then opened her mouth and took my nipple into her mouth. It felt so good. I started to moan. She could hear how good it felt to me, so she started to grind harder on me. I began to grind her back, but then began to lose control of my body with excitement going through me. I felt something happening to my body. I had no idea what was going on. I got scared and pushed her off of me in a sudden rush.

She said, "What's wrong, Carrie? Was I hurting you?"

But I was stunned so I said, "No, everything is fine."

"Then why did you push me off of you?"

In a panic I said, "I don't know; something was happening inside of me."

"Awe, baby, you were having an orgasm."

"Well, it scared me. I'm sorry."

"Carrie, it's okay." She started to hold me in her arms. Since I had never had a sex talk with my mom, I had to learn everything by doing it. "Carrie, I want you to know how much I love you. I'll never cheat on you and I'll always be here for you. We can take things slow. If you want to just be friends, then that's okay too. But if you get a boyfriend or a girlfriend, I can't watch that. I'm sorry, Carrie, but I would have to stay away from that because I already love you too much to see you with someone else."

"Kim, I like being your girlfriend. I want to be your girlfriend forever. I love you."

Kim shocked me when she said, "Carrie, you can be my girlfriend for now, but in time, I want to make you my wife."

I had never felt happier, I told her I wanted that too. She held me the rest of the night. I would never forget it. It was my first time having sex, my first orgasm, and also the first time I ever really felt that someone really loved me. No one ever forgets their first time, whether it was good or bad. Fortunately for me, my experience with Kim was wonderful.

The next day was Saturday and I was feeling kind of shy but excited at the same time. We had planned to spend that night watching a movie she wanted me to see called *Two Girls in Love*. We made our pallet on the floor, got our junk food, and put the movie in. It was a cute movie. It made me feel as if I was going through the same thing the girls were going through in the movie. It was about two young girls in high school falling in love with each other, caught up in their own little world. As we watched the movie, Kim would softly caress me and kiss my ear and neck. When the movie ended, we began to kiss.

Kim was so gentle with me. She slipped off my pajama top and began to caress my nipple. She very softly took the tip of my nipple into her mouth, swirling her tongue all around it as I began to tingle. Slowly, she slipped her hand into my pajama bottoms, playing with my clitoris, feeling my wetness, sliding inside of me. I began to shiver as she kissed down my stomach. She slipped my bottoms off, and then kissed my inner thigh. And then, it happened. Her tongue entered my insides, filling me with pleasure. I let out a loud sigh as her tongue got deeper and deeper, then her lips wrapped around my clitoris. She began to suck on it. I couldn't control my body as it began to shiver more. As I started to thrust my pelvis, she was right there, matching my rhythm, and it felt good. I knew I was about to cum. I was completely taken by what she was doing to me and shouted, "Oh Kim, I love you! I'm going to cum!" It happened. I was shaking, shivering, and I had lost all control of my body. I felt like I gave all of me to her. She was now the only person who could control how good my body felt. I knew at that point, I could not live without Kim, nor did I want to. She was the girl with whom I planned on living my life.

The next day I was so happy, I walked around grinning all day. It was my new life and there was no way I was going to let Kim get away from me. We spent so much time together; it was like we were joined at the hip. The only time we spent apart was when we went to our separate classes or when I went home, which wasn't very often. My favorite time was when we just lied in bed after making love, her caressing me, telling me how much she loved me and that she would never leave me. It was comforting to hear her say she would always be there for me. Nothing made me happier than being with Kim. We talked about the future and how we would grow old together, how we would live for us and not care what people thought about us as a couple. We agreed it wouldn't be our problem if other people didn't like seeing two girls in love, which was kind of funny, considering we were hiding it from our moms. I was so far gone, Kim could have told me anything and I would have believed it. I would go anywhere with her and knew that I wanted to be with her always. She seemed to be fulfilling all of my needs for the love I never had growing up. I no longer felt alone. When we were seniors, I decided it was time to ask who C.J. was. We were sitting in Kim's backyard. She was trying to talk me into swimming or allowing her to teach me how to swim. I would only put my feet in the pool while she swam around. I finally got the guts to ask her about C.J.

"Kim, I really want to ask you something, and I hope it's not too personal or something you don't want to talk about."

She swam over to me and said, "Okay, Carrie, what do you want to ask me?"

I took a deep breath and said, "Who is C.J?"

She just looked at me and very calmly said, "C.J. was my first love. Her name is Camie James."

I said, "What happened to her? I mean, why aren't you with her anymore? Of course, I'm happy you're not, because then I wouldn't have you all to myself." I took her hand and held it as I said that.

"Well, Camie and I were kind of like you and I," she said, "until one night when we were making out in her room and her mother walked in on us. Her mom made sure I wouldn't see Camie anymore. Her family was very religious, so her parents sent her away to boarding school, and I haven't seen her since that day. That was about three years ago."

I said, "Wow, so you were only fourteen. That's kind of young."

"Carrie, we weren't exactly having sex. We would just kiss and make out a little. We spent a lot of time together, and we loved each other very much."

"So you never heard from her again? Didn't she write you or try to call you?"

"Nope, I never heard from her again."

"I'm sorry, Kim. That must have been hard."

"Yes, it was, but I don't want to talk about it anymore. I'm with you now and I'm going to spend my life with you."

I was left to wonder if she still missed C.J. or if she still loved her, but I didn't ask. Instead I asked Kim if I could spend the following Saturday with her and she agreed to let me. It was very important to me that she didn't make any other plans.

"Kim, would you mind if we spent it at your house?"

She agreed but then asked "Why are you asking? We spend all of our weekends together." I told her it was my birthday and that I never had a birthday party. I let her know that I just didn't want to spend another birthday alone.

"Oh my god, why didn't you tell me it was your birthday? It's bad enough I missed it last year."

"Because I never celebrate it. My mom really doesn't do anything. If I bring it up to her, she just says it was the worst day of her life. She says if I can find one person that's happy I was born, then we can celebrate it. So I don't really think about it or bring it up to anyone."

I could see tears welling up in Kim's eyes when I told her that. By now she knew how bad my mother treated me. She got out of the pool, walked over to me, hugged me, and said, "Don't make any other plans on Saturday."

When I told my mom I would be spending next Saturday at Kim's house because it was my birthday, she said, "Oh, you mean hell day!" You would think my mom won a prize every time she put me down, she did it so often. When she said that, I just put my head down and went to my room.

I had spent the night before my birthday with Kim. In the morning, I was woken up to a special birthday breakfast from Kim. She brought in a tray of all my favorites, . with a card sitting on the tray. On the outside of the card, it said, "Happy Birthday." On the inside, Kim had written:

> This is a very special day to me.
> This is the day my girl was born for me.
> I'm very thankful and happy that my girl was born on this day.
> Happy Birthday, baby.
>
> Love,
> Your girl Kim…

I had tears coming down each side of my face when I read the card. I said, "Thank you, babe. That wasn't only my first birthday card, but it was the most beautiful card I have ever read."

Kim kissed me and said, "This is just the beginning of your birthday." Then, she fed me breakfast in bed.

We got dressed, and then Kim drove us to Disneyland. We had such a good time; we took lots of pictures and went on so many rides together. I had never been to Disneyland so I was in awe the whole time. We got home around 8 p.m. and I was exhausted. When we got to the house, Kim and I went to her room to lie down. A few minutes later, Kim's mom called us to come downstairs. Kim ran down and I walked, so when I got to the dining room, they were standing there with a cake and seventeen candles singing "Happy Birthday." All I could do was cry. It was the most beautiful cake I had ever seen, and to think it was for me. That completely surprised me; it was something I never had before.

After I blew out the candles, Kim's mom handed me a very pretty wrapped box and said, "Happy Birthday, Carrie."

I said, "Thank you," with tears still coming down my face. Kim got me some tissue and tried to wipe my tears, but they just kept flowing. I opened the present, and inside were these pretty silver earrings. I hugged Kim's mom and said, "Thank you so much!" Then Kim handed me a small wrapped present. When I opened it, inside was a beautiful necklace to match the earrings Kim's mom had given me. I wanted to kiss Kim, but I just hugged her instead. I thanked Kim and her mother for such a wonderful birthday. Kim's mom said she had to go out and wouldn't be back until late afternoon the next day. Looking back, I think she was just trying to give Kim and me some time alone on my birthday. Of course we made love all night. After that Kim, made sure I had the best birthdays every year.

Chapter Four

The Plans We Made

We had planned on going to college together and I could not wait. Freedom is all we could think of. No more sneaking around or waiting until Kim's mother went out of town or even waiting until we thought she was asleep before we made love. We had both been accepted into San Diego State. Thank God I got a full scholarship. I was a straight-A student all through high school, knowing my mom wasn't going to help me with college. I got offers to other colleges, which some people would say I was stupid for turning down, but I was going wherever Kim went.

High school graduation day came, and I was hoping my mother would come, but like all my other graduations, she told me at the last minute that she had plans with her boyfriend and wasn't going to be there. I had made a point to tell my mom three weeks before graduation that I was going to be class valedictorian, but I guess it didn't encourage her enough to come.

Kim's mom was there, of course and took both of us out afterward. Kim's graduation gift was an American Express card, so she could get what she wanted while living in San Diego. Kim's mom asked me where my mother was and because I felt ashamed, I lied and said she had to work.

"I'm sorry," she said. "Wow, she couldn't get off for your speech? By the way, it was very good and I'm very proud of you."

It made me happy hearing her say that. I only wish my mother felt that way. "Thank you," I said.

The following weekend we had planned on going down to San Diego to look at some apartments. I remember the first time we went to check out the campus. It was like we were grownups. We made plans to get our own apartment, two bedrooms in case our parents wanted to visit. That was my idea. My plan was to get a part-time job so that I could pay my half of the rent. Kim told me her mother had given her a budget, so she was able to afford a two-bedroom apartment without needing my help. Kim wanted us to have more time to study and more time with each other.

So for the first week of summer, we set out to find our own apartment in San Diego, just me and my girl. It was so much fun. We stayed in a hotel in Mission Valley, and I don't have to tell you we spent a lot of time in the room. We also went shopping at the mall and tried to get into some Lesbian bar called The Flame, up in Hillcrest, but they were really strict with IDs. We were too young to get in, but it was still fun trying. By Sunday, we finally set out to look for an apartment close to campus. There were some dumps, some really upscale places, and some that were nice. We figured we would have to come back a few more times before we found something we really liked.

About the fourth time out, Kim's mom decided that she would come out and help us look. Amazingly, we found a place on the first day she came with us. It's funny how you can find what you need when you're not making love, shopping, or trying to get into bars. It was a really nice place, so our next stop was to go shopping for things that would make our apartment cute. Since my mom was so caught up in her new boyfriend, she was happy to have the house to herself.

I could not sleep the night before we moved in. Kim and I decided not to spend the night with each other. We wanted to make it that much more exciting when we did move in with each other for the first time, for what we thought was our forever.

The next morning, I said my good-byes to my mom as she and her new boyfriend were headed to the racetracks. I was so happy to know I was moving in with Kim, so I didn't care that the only thing my mom said to me was "Good-bye, and don't call me for money." I jumped in the car with Kim and her mom, then off we went on our drive down to San Diego. We spent the day getting settled in, and right after the moving people left, Kim's mom took us out to dinner. She gave Kim the rules of being on her own. Kim knew once her mom was gone, she would get to do what she wanted. I think Kim's mom knew that too, but being a parent, she always had to lay down some rules. She knew Kim was a good girl.

After dinner, Kim's mom took us grocery shopping. I was having so much fun when Kim said, "Remind me to never let you do the food shopping by yourself, because we would have nothing but junk food." I didn't really know what to get, other than things that went into a microwave and peanut butter sandwiches, along with cereal. My mom never cooked, so I never learned how to.

When we got back to the apartment, we put the groceries away, and then we both kissed Kim's mom good-bye. Kim's mom was crying and saying, "I can't believe my baby is all grown up and living on her own."

I was so jealous. I wanted my mother to care about me that way, but my mom didn't care about me at all. After Kim's mom left, we both screamed with joy. We were now on our own and we felt like we were free. First, we began by taking a shower together. Then we took it to the room. It was our first night on our own and we could do whatever we wanted without worrying about anyone walking in on us. So I decided to get creative.

I got up out of bed and went into the kitchen. It was dark, with just a little light coming through the blinds from the kitchen window. I called for Kim to come in and when she walked in, I was sitting on the counter. A big smile came across her face. I straddled her then pulled her into my breast. She was going at it on my nipples when I said, "Kim, slow down, baby. We have all night."

She said, "I know, but I have been waiting for this night all summer. I can't believe we live together. You're my wife and I love you so much, Carrie."

"I'm not going anywhere, Kim. I'm all yours forever, so let's try something new."

I jumped down and got an ice cube out of the freezer. Slowly, I turned Kim around and ran the ice cube down her back, then back up to the middle of her back as she shivered. I turned her back around, took the ice cube into my mouth then gently put my mouth on her nipple, swirling it around. She was in awe. I came back up with the ice cube still in my mouth. I began to kiss her neck. Then I worked my way down. For the first time, I went down on Kim with the ice cube while she leaned against the counter. She tasted so good. I had no idea what I was doing, but she loved it. Then it happened—I felt her body shake while she whispered my name as she climaxed.

The next morning, we made breakfast together, and then made love. We made lunch together, and then we made love. Finally we took a nap. A few hours later, we woke up to music playing next door that we could hear through the walls. Needless to say, it didn't bother us and we were happy in our cute apartment. We got up and took a shower—together, of course—then made dinner.

That night while we were lying in bed, all of a sudden Kim told me to get up. She put a CD in the CD player and said, "Dance with me." The song was "The Way You Look Tonight." One of the things I loved about Kim was that she didn't just like old movies. Like me, she also loved old music. She held me close and whispered in my ear, "I don't even think you know how much I love you."

Oh, to be young again! We had such a good time living together for our first year there. It was so unforgettable. I can't even begin to put it into words, but those who have been through it know what I'm talking about. It felt like nothing in the world could stop us. By then, we had been together three years. By the next year, we decided to join some gay groups and make new friends, that's when everything started to change.

Chapter Five

The College Years

Kim started going out all the time. She was going to clubs, and I would sometimes pop in and surprise her. She was always surrounded by girls. Although Kim would always grab my hand, pull me into her, and kiss me in front of the other girls, I still didn't like her being there with them. Women are very shady. One night, I showed up and Kim was dancing with some girl I had never seen. She didn't see me. I just stood there and watched her until she saw me. It wasn't until her friend, who was dancing with some other girl, tapped her on the shoulder and pointed at me as if to say, *There's Carrie.* When Kim waved to me, I turned around and left. Kim ran after me and when she caught up to me she said, "What's wrong, babe?"

"What do you mean what's wrong? Who is that you were dancing with?"

"I don't know, some girl."

"So, this is what you want now, Kim?"

"What are you talking about, Carrie? I told you I wanted to go dancing. You said you didn't want to go, and that it was okay for me to go. What did you think? I just wanted to watch people dance?"

"Kim!"

"Carrie!"

"Okay, fine, Kim! I'll just move out and you can party all the time and go out with as many girls as you want!" I started to walk away. People were watching us have this conversation outside of the club.

Kim grabbed my hand and said, "I don't know how many times I have to tell you, I only want you, babe. All I was doing was dancing. I wasn't even slow dancing, but if you don't want me to dance with anyone else, then I won't. I'll just wait until you're in the mood, okay, babe?"

"Kim, I think I should move out and let you do your thing. Maybe you need to date different girls. I mean, they all want you and maybe deep down inside you want that, but I'm holding you back. You have been going out a lot lately. I feel like you don't want me around anymore and maybe you need to explore this, to make sure this is what you really want." Feeling hurt, I said, "Maybe you don't want me anymore."

"Babe, don't ever say that. I love you. Why would you say that?"

"Kim, you're never home anymore!"

Kim looked at me and said, "Carrie, why don't we start doing things together, okay?"

"I don't know, Kim. I mean, look at you. You're a very pretty girl and all those girls want you. Don't you want to try having some fun?"

"Babe, I have fun with you. I want to be with you. Look, I just wanted to go out and dance. You said you didn't want to go and that you were okay with it. If I thought you were going to get upset, I wouldn't have come." I just stood there looking at her, and thinking I knew she had to love the attention she got from all those girls. "Carrie, say something?"

"Kim, I don't know what to say."

"Carrie, please don't do this."

"What am I doing?"

"You're trying to break up with me, because you think I want to be with a bunch of girls and that could not be further from the truth."

"Kim, what am I suppose to think? I mean, how would you feel if every time you went out with me, a bunch of girls were after me? Or every time you weren't around, a bunch of girls sent me drinks, trying to get in my pants?"

"If I knew you loved me as much as I love you, I wouldn't worry about it."

"Kim, I'm not mad. I just think we need a break from each other. Then that way you can get out there and make sure you really know what you want."

"Carrie, don't do this. I have what I want, babe."

"I'm just trying to make sure you're happy, Kim. Maybe after you date a few girls, you'll know for sure." Kim was getting visibly angry.

"Carrie, I'm not doing that!"

"Babe, look, I'll call a friend and maybe stay with her for a while. This way you can do what you need to do. I'll see you later."

I was surprised when Kim got mad and said, "Okay, that's it! Carrie, I let you get away with a lot of shit, but I'll be damned if you're leaving me. I don't want to date those fucking girls! They're out there looking for what I already have. This is bullshit! Where's your car?"

Everyone was looking at us as Kim yelled at me. I pointed to my car. Kim grabbed my hand and took me to my car, walking really fast. When we got to my car, she took me to the passenger's side and said, "Give me your keys!" She was very forceful, so I gave them to her. She opened my door and told me to get in, so I did. She got in on the driver's side and started to drive.

I said, "Kim, where are we going and what about your car?"

She didn't say anything. We pulled into a dark park that was up the street from the club. She got out and walked around to my side of the car to open my door. "Get out!" she said with strong conviction.

I was somewhat afraid, but I did what she said. She opened the back door, forced me down in the backseat, pulled my skirt up, pulled down my panties, pulled down her pants, and laid on top of me. She started grinding me and it felt so good. When I started moaning, she asked, "Do you feel that?"

"Yes."

"Does this feel like I want someone else?"

"No, baby!"

"Do you want me, Carrie?"

I was feeling really good and quickly answered, "Yes, baby, I want, I want you."

She put two of her fingers inside of me, and as she massaged my insides, she said, "Does this feel like I want you?"

"Yes, baby, it does!"

"Are you going to leave me?"

"No, baby." Still tingling and feeling good, I said, "I promise I'm not going anywhere."

"Then prove it to me!"

I softly whispered, "What do you want me to do, baby?"

"Cum for me right now, Carrie. Show me you want me and only me!"

It was feeling so good that I felt myself exploding. "I'm Cumming, right now! Oh, Kim, I love you!" I had never seen Kim be so forceful. It was such a turn on and I loved it!

After that, Kim and I started going to different places together. We were meeting with all kinds of girl groups, going to parties, and that's when we started letting people into our so-called world.

Chapter Six

Something Just Doesn't Feel Right

We met this girl at the gay and lesbian center; her name was Michelle. She was tall, pretty, and had a smile that could melt anyone's heart. Although she was pretty, she had that tomboy thing going on with her. She had dark brown hair and green eyes. About two months after we met her, I noticed that Michelle was taking a liking to Kim. At first I thought she was a nice person who wanted to be friends. She would hang out at our apartment with us, and when it came time to go to bed, Kim would have her sleep in our spare room because of all the wine we would drink, which became a bad habit. One day after coming home from school, I found Michelle in our home with Kim; I got this weird feeling. You know the kind you get when something doesn't feel right? The kind that gives you bad butterflies in your stomach?

"Hi, babe," I said to Kim as I walked in and gave her a kiss.

She said, "How was class?"

"It was good," I said. "How was your day?"

"It was fun. Michelle and I went down to the beach. We got in the water for a while. We decided to layout and get some sun. After that, we had a nice lunch. We just got back about thirty minutes ago."

Needless to say, I was jealous but tried not to show it. I said, "What are we doing for dinner, babe?"

"Michelle thought we should try out this new place called Spices."

"Okay, if that's where you want to go."

"You don't want to go there, Carrie?"

"No, we can go; whatever you want to do, Kim, is fine with me."

"Good," Kim said, "because Michelle is dying to try their food."

All I could think was *Great. Michelle is going.* It seemed lately I could not get any alone time with Kim, whether it was going to lunch, dinner, or at home. Something just didn't seem right, but I didn't want to say anything to Kim about it. I didn't want her to think I was being possessive. After all, she was so happy having a new friend. I just went along with everything, waiting for some alone time with Kim. It seemed like it would never come.

Two months passed and still, she wasn't giving us any time alone. Christmas was coming soon and we were going home. I figured I would get some time with her alone then. Kim's mom had bought her a new car halfway through our first year of college and I was driving her old car, which wasn't so old. I know Kim—that was her way of making sure I had what she had. I couldn't wait until our drive home alone, just Kim and I.

As we were packing the car, Michelle pulled up in her car and said, "I'm ready." I know the look on my face could not be hidden.

"Is there something wrong?" Kim said to me.

I pulled Kim aside and said, "You didn't tell me she was coming with us. Why didn't you tell me?"

She said, "I didn't think you would mind."

"Kim, it's been a long time since we had any time together alone and I was counting on this time with you. It seems like she's always with us or with you. What's going on, Kim?"

"She's our friend, Carrie."

"No, she's your friend, Kim, and I don't trust her. Something is just not right. Is there something you want to tell me, Kim?"

"What do you mean, Carrie?"

"You know what I'm talking about, Kim. Don't play dumb."

"Look, she's walking up now so be nice, and we'll talk about this later."

"No, we need to talk about this now or I'm not going!"

Kim said in a whisper to me, "Let's go inside." Then she told Michelle to put her stuff in the car and that we would be right back. As we entered the house, I slammed the door behind me. Kim looked stunned. She said, "What is wrong with you, Carrie? Why are you acting like this?"

"I need you to tell me where she's staying, Kim."

"What do you mean, where is she staying? I invited her, so she will be staying with me. She didn't want to go home to all of that cold weather in Ohio for Christmas."

"So you invited her to stay with you, all alone? That's great. Okay, so is there something going on between you two that I don't know about?"

"What are you suggesting, Carrie?"

"I'm suggesting that I see the way she looks at you. It's been three months and we have had no alone time and we haven't made love in a very long time. You have to be getting something out of your time with her. If you don't want me anymore, I would like you to tell me now! You know what? Just forget it! I'm not going. I'll just stay here and pack my stuff. When you get back from L.A, I'll be gone out of your life."

"I have no idea where all of this is coming from, Carrie, but it's not true. I want you and I'm not doing anything that I shouldn't be doing. Carrie, I love you and always will. I promise I'll make time for just you, and soon! It's just that you know I'll be without my mom while we're at home, so she's going to keep me company. Come on, Carrie, don't you trust me?"

"It's not you that I don't trust, it's her."

Kim said, "Look at me, Carrie." And I did. "I love you and only you. I want you and only you. Got it?"

"Fine, Kim."

"Tell me you love me, Carrie!"

"No!"

"Carrie, if you love me, I want to hear you say it right now." I didn't say anything. She took my hand and said, "Come on, Carrie. Don't make me put you in the backseat of the car again."

Little did she know that wasn't a threat since it had been so long since she and I had made love, I wanted her to throw me down in the backseat and show me how much she wanted me. But I just said, "Yes, you know I love you."

She kissed me and said, "You're so silly sometimes."

We started our drive home and deep down inside, I wasn't happy, I knew that it wasn't going to be a nice homecoming, with me worrying if something was going on while they were alone. When I got home, it seemed like I called Kim every five minutes just to stop something that might possibly be going on between the two of them.

So many things were going on in my head. What were they doing? Where was Michelle sleeping? Did she make a move on Kim? Would Kim fall in love with Michelle after spending all that time alone with her, like she did with me? I began to go crazy.

At one point, my mom even asked, "Are you okay? You don't seem very happy."

But I just blew her off by saying, "I'm just tired." It wasn't like she really cared anyway so I didn't care to talk about it with her.

I decided to stop calling Kim every few minutes and take a nap. A few hours later, my mom called me in for one of her famous TV dinners. I just sat there, not in the mood to eat. My stomach was in knots. I hadn't heard from Kim, and I had no idea what I was going to do if there was something going on. I sat and listened to music, thinking about more crazy things that could be happening between the two of them. Why hadn't she just left me in San Diego? I could have just packed my stuff and moved out so she and Michelle could be together with no problems from me.

I decided to take a walk. I found myself in front of Kim's house, wondering what they were doing inside. Was this the end of us? Would I die of heartbreak? It sure felt that way. I didn't go to the door. I just walked back home and waited for Kim to call. I wasn't going to call anymore. I had made up my mind. When we got back to San Diego, I would pack my stuff and leave. She hadn't called me and I was so hurt. One hour passed and no call from Kim. Then two hours. Then four hours. Next thing I knew, I was waking up the next morning and I hadn't received one single call all night. I knew it was going to be a bad day.

As far as I could tell, she had forgotten all about me within two days. We had never gone this long without talking. I was so hurt, that it truly felt like I could barely breathe. What was I going to do having to see her at school? Where would I live? It was too late to move into a dorm and I couldn't afford an apartment on my own. I didn't know what I was going to do, but I knew I would be packing as soon as we got back. How could I handle seeing Kim walking around school knowing she had a new girlfriend? I knew I was going to die! There was nothing else I could do. I was going to let my heart slowly die of heartbreak. I didn't want to see any of it unfold. I kept asking myself, how could Kim do this to me? Was it that easy for her to fall out of love with me?

It was Christmas Day and I was spending it at my mom's house with no tree, no decorations, and certainly no Christmas dinner.

Around 3 p.m. Mom said, "I'm headed out. I'll be home in the morning. There are some TV dinners in the refrigerator." Then she left. No "Merry Christmas," no presents, not even a card, but it was like that with her growing up so no surprise there.

I sat and tried to watch TV, but I kept thinking about Kim and Michelle together. Then it happened. Finally Kim called. I couldn't decide if I should answer it and let her break my heart, or if I should ignore it. I couldn't resist. I answered it, but in a very cold way.

"Hello," she said. "Carrie?"

I pretended I didn't know it was her. I said, "Yes, who's calling?"

She started laughing and said, "Merry Christmas! It's me, Kim." She was still laughing when she said, "Oh, now you don't know my voice? That's very funny, Carrie."

I was very standoffish. I said, "Is there something you need, Kim?"

"Come on, babe," Kim said. "Don't do this again. I need to talk to you. It's very important."

I said, "Well, after not hearing from you for three days, I'm listening."

"No, I need you to come over tonight at seven," she said. "Do you think you can do this?"

"Oh, now you have time for me?"

"I know, Carrie. I've been busy, but I really need you to come over tonight at seven."

"Whatever you need to tell me you can tell me now."

"Babe, come on."

"Fine, I'll see you tonight."

"Do you need me to pick you up?"

I said in a very cold, sarcastic tone, "No, I'll get there on my own, the way I've been for the last three days."

"Carrie, I'm sorry. We just need to talk."

"Yes, I'm sure you have a lot to tell me, Kim."

"I'll see you at seven, babe."

I walked to Kim's house; I had a lot to think about. Like what was I going to do once she told me she was in love with Michelle and no longer wanted to be with me? Would she just move me out? Where would I stay? Could I stay with a friend until I could afford my own place? So many things were going through my mind. But then when I really thought about it, I was going to die of heartbreak anyway, so it really didn't even matter.

At 7 p.m., I rang Kim's doorbell, and I could hear footsteps coming toward the door. When she opened it, she was dressed nice. She looked so pretty. I had to hold my ground and not comment, pretending not to notice. After all, this was the woman who was about to break my heart.

She reached out and gently took my hand to pull me into her. She kissed me softly, hugged me real tight, and said, "I've missed you so much."

I was so confused. She held my hand as she led me to the dining room, where the lights were off. Candles lit the entire room. The table was set with a nice dinner waiting, and soft music was playing. She said, "I need you to just listen to me before we eat. I want to ask you something."

"Wait, who said I was staying for dinner? And why should I?"

"You're staying because you love me." She started kissing me and saying, "Don't you, baby?"

I could never resist her. I said, "Yes."

She then stood in front of me, pulled out a pretty gift wrapped box, and said, "Open it."

I said, "But Kim, don't you want to talk?"

"Yes, this is what I want to talk about. Open it!"

So I did. Inside was a beautiful ring. She got down on one knee and said, "Will you marry me?"

I turned to her and said, "But what about you and Michelle?"

"Babe, that's why I wanted her here. She helped me pick out the ring and helped me set everything up for tonight."

"Oh my God, I feel so stupid."

"It's okay, Carrie. I understand. I was planning this for months and that's why Michelle and I were spending so much time together. I wanted everything to be perfect for us. Do have any idea how many jewelry stores we went to just to find the right ring for you? Babe, I love you and I'll never cheat on you. Carrie, you are my life and whatever I do, it will always involve you. Don't you know you're the love of my life? Even though the law doesn't recognize our love, that doesn't mean I don't. I want to marry you."

"I'm sorry, babe, I'm really sorry. I thought I was losing you. I just knew I was going to die without you. Is Michelle upstairs? I want to apologize to her."

"Well, you're going to have to wait until we get back to San Diego. She got on a plane this morning to Ohio."

"I feel so bad, Kim."

"It's okay. She felt bad because of the way you were feeling, so she wanted me to tell you, she didn't want you to hate her."

"Okay. I'm going to have to get her something to make it up to her."

"Carrie, you never answered me. Will you marry me?"

With a big smile on my face, I said, "Yes, Kim, a million times yes, I will!"

She kissed me. I knew she loved me at that point. I had no doubt.

She hugged me and said, "I love you so much, babe. I want to spend my life with you. I want to spend the rest of my life making you smile!" Then she said, "Okay, well, I hope you're hungry because I've been slaving over the stove ever since I got back from dropping Michelle off at the airport."

"Yes, I am. I love you so much, Kim." I hugged her tightly and said, "Did you make this all by yourself?"

"Yes, I did, with a few tips from Rosa. She has been showing me how to make this for the last few days. That's why I didn't call you. Plus, you know I can't stand to hear you or see you sad. If I would have talked to you, I would have broken down and ruined the surprise." Kim led me to my seat and said, "Now dig in, and then you need to call your mother and tell her you're going to spend the night, because I'm going to dig into you tonight. It's been a long time since I had a taste of you."

"Oh yeah? Well, do you remember that night in the backseat of my car?"

"Yes, very well." She says with a smile on her face

"Well, it's payback time." I got up and straddled Kim's lap. Then I took her fork and started feeding her. Every time she took a bite, she had to give me a kiss. I slipped down to her lap, unsnapped the buttons on her pants, and then slowly slipped them off. I said, "Open your legs."

She said, "Babe, what are you doing?"

"Don't you think you should do what your wife asks of you, or do you want to pay the price?"

She opened her legs, took my hand, and slid it into her panties. With two fingers, I went deep inside of her. I could tell she was really turned on. She was really wet. I said, "Do you love me, Kim?"

She said, "Baby what are you doing to me?"

"Just answer me, Kim."

"Yes, baby, I . . . I . . . love you." I guess she was feeling good because she could barely speak.

"Kim, I think you have been a very bad girl staying away from me that long."

She whispered, "I know, baby, but—"

I said, "But what, Kim? Do you think it's okay to not call me or not come see me for that long?"

She said, "Baby, I love you."

"Show me that you love me, Kim."

"What do you want me to do?" she asked. She could barely speak.

I started messing around with her and said, "What, Kim? I don't understand what you're saying?"

She whispered again, this time saying, "Baby, what are you doing to me?"

I said, "I'm making my wife feel as good as she just made me feel when she asked me to marry her."

She gently moaned. "Oh, this feels so good." And then I slid my tongue deep inside of her. She grabbed the back of my hair really hard and said, "Baby, I love you so much. I'll do anything you want me to do! Oh my God, oh my God, I . . . I . . . I love you!"

Let's just say that was the best dinner I ever had.

The next day, Kim and I spent the whole day in bed. We made love like it was going out of style. I made her punish me a lot.

Over the next three years, Kim kept bugging me about getting married. I wanted to wait until the law changed in California. By our last year in school, we had met so many people at the gay center and at school that we felt like we owned the town. We had grown into young women. And we had been together eight years at that point. Kim was going to be a counselor for young gay teens and I was going to be a writer. I had nothing that I really wanted to write about, but I said one day I was going to sit down and write all of my life stories.

Graduation was coming up soon. Since we planned on living together, we thought it was only right that we told our parents about our relationship. So Kim called her mother since she could never catch her at home. Her mother took the news really well. As a matter of fact, her mother said she already knew; she was just waiting for Kim to tell her. But she also said to Kim, "I have one question for you."

Kim said, "Okay, Mom, what is it?"

"Are you happy, Kim?"

"I could not be happier," Kim told her.

"That's all I care about."

It was now my turn to get the courage to tell my mom. I was scared. You see, Kim's mom was really understanding about everything she did. I decided I was going to tell my mom in person, so my plan was to go to L.A. for the weekend. Kim would drive and keep me calm on the drive up there. I didn't know what to expect. We had never had that mother-daughter talk and we weren't the type of household that ever talked about sex. Hell, who was I kidding? My mom hardly ever talked to me about anything.

Kim dropped me off, went to her house, and waited for my call. As I approached the door, I felt my legs getting weak. I was so nervous. I opened the door and said, "I'm home!"

I had called my mom to let her know I had something to talk to her about, so she would make time for me. When I heard no response, I looked around for my mom. I walked into her room without knocking first; I was shocked to see her in there with her latest boyfriend. I quickly closed the door and waited in the living room for my mom to come out. It wasn't until an hour later that I realized she wasn't coming out anytime soon. I went into my room and called Kim to let her know what was going on.

Kim said, "I'll come pick you up and we'll go get something to eat."

While we were out, I decided to call my mom to ask her when she would have time for our talk, but she didn't pick up. After we finished eating, Kim took me back to her house. We talked and listened to music for a while. Around eight, she dropped me back off at my house, where my mom was sitting at the dining room table with her new boyfriend, eating dinner.

"Hey Mom," I said. "Sorry about earlier. How are you?"

She waved and said, "What do you want?"

"I would like to talk to you about my plans after I graduate."

"I hope you're not going to ask for money, because I don't have any." She always reminded me of that.

I said, "No, I don't need any money."

"Well, what is it that you want?"

"Just a few minutes of your time, and some understanding."

"What is it that you want me to understand?"

"Mom, do you think I could speak to you alone? This is hard enough just telling you."

"Anything you can say to me you can say to James. Just say it."

"Maybe I'll talk to you when you have some alone time for me." James was just sitting there looking at me. I didn't even know this man, had never even met him, and she wanted me to tell her my personal business in front of him.

Mom said, "Well, he lives here now so that's going to be hard. Just tell us what's on your mind."

"Mom, I came here all the way from San Diego to talk to you. Can't you give me a few minutes of your time?"

She didn't even try to make an effort to talk to me alone. Instead, she said, "Tell me what you have to talk to me about Carrie."

"That's okay, Mom. I'll talk to you another time."

I went to my room and called Kim. I told her what happened, then asked her to come and pick me up. She took me back to her house and the next day we went back to San Diego, without me telling my mom.

Graduation day was a few weeks later. Right before we headed out the door, I called to see if my mom was on her way. She told me she would not be coming because she had plans to go to the racetrack with James. I was hurt, of course, but not surprised. This was typical and as usual, other things were still more important to her than my graduation.

When I told Kim, she was very disappointed and reassured me she would be here for me for the rest of my life. She said, "I'm sorry, babe, but my mom will be here for the both of us."

I smiled and said, "Thanks," but I could still feel the pain I felt all the way back to my first kindergarten graduation, when I stood on that stage all by myself. As we sat and listened during our graduation ceremony, I felt the tears welling up in my eyes, thinking of my mom not being here for me. Kim saw the tears in my eyes, held my hand, and said, "It's going to be okay. I'm here."

I always wondered what I did to make my mom hate me so much. I felt like she hated me all of my life. I began to think maybe my father did know I existed and that when he found out Mom was pregnant, maybe she blamed me for him leaving her. It made sense.

After graduation, Kim's mom took us out to eat. While we were sitting there, Kim's mom said, "Where's your mom?"

Before I could answer, Kim said, "She couldn't get off work!"

"I'm sorry," Kim's mom said.

"It's okay," I said.

Kim's mom then handed her a really pretty wrapped box and said, "Happy Graduation, baby."

Kim got up, hugged her mom, and said, "Thank you! What is it?"

Her mom said, "Open it, silly." Inside was a platinum credit card. "I got you that card so that you won't have any problems taking care of yourself and your girl.

Kim said, "Thank you, Mom. I love you!"

"You're so welcome, baby. I'm very proud of you. Carrie, I'm very proud of you, too." Then she handed Kim another box. Inside was a gold heart on a chain with an empty spot where a key went.

"Well, Mom," Kim said, "where's the key?"

Kim's mom handed me a pretty wrapped box and said, "Happy Graduation, Carrie."

I could not believe it! She had gotten me something. Inside was the missing key on a very pretty chain. I started bawling.

Her mom said, "Carrie, what's wrong? Don't you like it?"

Kim put her arm around me and said, "Mom, it's her first graduation gift ever. Her mom has never shown up for any of her graduations and hasn't ever gotten anything for her."

Her mom said, "I'm so sorry about that. I didn't mean to upset you. I just wanted to get my girls something special."

After wiping my eyes, I said, "I'm sorry. I'll be fine. Thank you very much." I gave Kim's mom a hug.

She then kissed me on the cheek and said, "You're so very welcome."

I'll never forget Kim's mom for what she did that day and the gift she gave me.

Later that night, Kim and I decided to hit some graduation parties. We had a great time and didn't come home until the next day. We were hung over and tired. The last thing I remember was taking my eighth shot. After that, I don't recall a thing. Since Michelle went with us and didn't drink, she kind of filled us in on the things we did. She had us laughing so hard that our heads were hurting. We had to tell her to stop. We were all in the living room, I had my head in Kim's lap, and Michelle was entertaining us. Michelle told us she had met a girl at the party and decided to tell us about her, instead of making our heads hurt more. She seemed to like this new girl, Angie, a lot, and had talked to her a few times at school, but now they were going on a date.

Chapter Seven

New Friends Aren't Always

Good Friends

Kim suggested that we have a dinner party so that we could check out Michelle's new friend. I was happy that Michelle met someone that she really liked. Even though Michelle always came across as a happy person, a part of her seemed lonely. So when she told us that she had met someone new, I was happy for her and hoped that everything would work out for her. We made a plan. Michelle's job was to find out her likes and dislikes in the food department. Our job was to go out, get a nice dinner, and provide some entertainment, like cards or board games—something that was mellow so we could ask her a bunch of questions about herself.

The night came for us to meet Michelle's new friend. When they arrived together, I immediately noticed she was very pretty. She was blond, petite, and had brown eyes. She acted as if she knew she was a pretty girl.

Kim took their coats, introduced herself, and then said, "This is my wife, Carrie."

I said, "Hi," then offered them both a glass of wine. It was a nice bottle of chardonnay. Michelle took each of their glasses and led them to the couch, where Kim was ready to ask all kinds of questions.

Kim said, "So Angie, where are you from?"

Angie said, "Miami, Florida, by way of New York. I grew up in New York and moved to Miami right after high school. I've been here for about three years and I graduate next year."

Kim said, "Oh what are you studying?"

She said, "I'm a Theater Art major."

Kim said, "Oh wow, my mom is an actress."

Angie said, "Oh, really? Would I have seen her in anything?"

"Right now, she does Broadway mostly. She had a part on a show called *Hollow's Way* when she was a teenager, along with a few other shows and a few movies."

Angie said, "What part did your mother play on *Hollow's Way*? I used to love that show. I used to watch the reruns all the time."

Kim said, "She was Mandy, the teenage daughter always getting into trouble!"

Angie got excited. She said, "Oh my God! Your mother is April Springs? She is one of my idols! What a small world."

Kim said, "I'll be sure to tell her I have a new friend who is a big fan."

Angie was so excited. She asked, "Does she ever come to visit you, and if she does, do you think I could meet her?"

Kim said, "She doesn't get here to see me too much with her busy schedule, although you just missed her. She was here for a few days for our graduation. If she does come and you're around, I'll do my best to let Michelle know."

Then Angie said, "Kim, do you do any acting? You're very pretty."

Kim said, "Thank you, but no. You can keep Hollywood, that's not for me."

I said, "Okay, everybody, dinner is ready. I hope everyone is hungry! Kim and I made a lot of food." Of course, Kim really cooked it all. We started with a salad, and then moved on to a nice salmon dinner. I asked, "Does anyone want any more wine?"

As the night progressed, we tried talking to Angie about different things, but everything led back to Kim's mom or how pretty Kim was. It was like she knew who Kim was before she met her, and she was trying to get in good with Kim so that she could meet her mother. Kim and I gave each other that look like something wasn't right. Everything she said was *April Springs this* or *April Springs that.*

Angie said, "Kim, you should really be in front of the camera."

Kim again politely said, "No, thank you. I would rather be in front of Carrie."

I laughed and said, "Baby, you're so silly."

She kissed me and said, "I love you."

The next day when we tried to talk to Michelle about Angie, all Michelle said was how pretty she was. Michelle could not see past Angie's looks, but Kim saw that Michelle was going to have to learn the hard way. Then it got to the point that every time Michelle came over, Angie was with her. She would not stop talking about Kim's mom. It was getting on my nerves, and I could see that it was really getting on Kim's nerves. Kim wanted to tell Michelle not to bring her over anymore, but she didn't want to hurt Michelle like that. She was so into Angie that she couldn't see that Angie was flirting with Kim, but I could and I wasn't happy about it!

It really became a problem when Angie just popped up at our house while Kim was home alone. When I got home and saw Angie sitting on the couch and I didn't see Michelle, I asked, "Where's Michelle?" I walked up to Kim, kissed her, and said, "Hi, babe."

When I did that, Angie made a noise like she was bothered. "I don't know," Angie said. "I have been looking for her all day. I thought she was over here."

Once I heard that, I tried calling Michelle on her cell phone. When Michelle answered, I said, "Michelle, where have you been all day?"

She said, "At work, and I'm trying to track Angie down." Michelle was now working as a makeup artist for a local TV show.

So I asked her, "Have you tried calling her cell phone?"

Michelle said, "Yes, I have been calling her cell phone all day, but it goes straight to voice mail."

I said, "Angie, where is your cell phone?"

She answered, "It's in my purse why?"

"Can I see it?" I asked.

She started to hand it to me then looks at it and said, "Oh, it's off now. How did that happen?"

I said, "I thought you said you have been calling Michelle all day?" I was angry at this point.

"I have been; I don't know what happened."

As if she believed her, Kim looked at me and said, "It's an honest mistake. Where's Michelle?"

I gave Kim the evil eye. At that point, she knew she was in trouble. I asked Michelle, "Where are you right now?"

"I'm at home."

I said, "Okay, I'll send Angie right over."

Angie said, "Why don't you have her come over here and we can all hang out?"

Kim said, "Not tonight. I want to spend it alone with my wife. I have something special planned for her. Kim knew I was pissed.

Angie said, "Oh, I'm sorry. It must be nice having someone treat you so well. I hope you appreciate your woman because if you don't, someone else will, if you know what I mean."

All I could think was *No, she didn't just say that!* There was no way I was going to let this bitch come in here and take Kim from me. I said, "Okay, that's it! You have to go now."

And as she walked out the door, she turned to Kim and said, "I hope to see you soon, and don't forget my offer."

I slammed the door behind her. I knew something wasn't right with that girl. I asked, "How long was she here, and what offer, Kim?" I was pissed and yelling at this point.

Kim said, "Calm down, babe, you know I don't want her."

"Did she try to touch you or kiss you? Kim, did you do something with her?"

Kim said, "Babe, come on, you know better than that!"

I stormed into the bedroom, slammed the door, and locked it.

Kim came to the door and said, "Let me in. Come on, babe. Open the door and I'll tell you what happened."

I yelled from the other side of the door, "Oh, so something did happen! I knew it!"

"No, babe, open the door, please."

"Why should I?"

"Come on, babe, you're being silly."

"Oh, I'm being silly? I come home to find you alone with Angie, she made you some offer, and I'm being silly?"

"Babe, please open the door."

I yelled, "No, go away!" I didn't listen to her, I told her to go sleep on the couch. Then I said, "Better yet, go sleep at Angie's house!" I threw my purse on the floor and lied down.

A few hours later, I woke up in the middle of the night. I knew I wasn't going to be able to sleep the whole night without Kim. I went into the kitchen for water and saw her sleeping on the couch. She looked so sweet lying there. I went over to her and started kissing her face. She woke up and I jumped up. Kim very sweetly asked me to sit back down.

She grabbed my hand and said, "Let me talk to you, please, babe. I don't want you to be upset. I love you, Carrie. You know I would never do anything to hurt you. I just need you to listen to me."

I didn't say anything. I sat back down, but I knew I wasn't going to like what I was about to hear.

"Babe, I know that you know Angie wasn't really looking for Michelle. When she got here she was acting kind of strange. I asked her to have a seat and that I would try to track down Michelle for her. Angie then said to me, 'Before you do that, do you have any more of that good wine that you served the first time I came over here?' I told her we were all out, although you know we always keep wine in the house. Then she started asking how long you and I have been together, so I told her. She also asked me if it ever gets boring and do I ever think about change, if I miss being single and free to date whoever I want. I told her no. I'm very much in love. She had the nerve to say, 'If you ever get bored, you know where I am.' That was the offer she was talking about. You know I would never want to date her, babe. I was about to ask her to leave after she said that, but then you walked in the door."

I said out loud, "That bitch! Kim, I'm getting tired of always having to worry about other women wanting you."

"Women don't always want me, but if there is something that I can do to make you feel better, I'll do it. Just tell me what you want me to do, Carrie."

"I don't know, Kim; I'm just saying it's getting old." I looked at Kim for a few minutes, got up, went back into the room, and locked the door. Kim started knocking at the door.

"Babe, please open the door. I know you hear me. Do you see what you're doing? You're letting someone come between us."

I opened the door and let her in, but then she tried hugging me so I pushed her away and said, "Why did you let her in?"

"Babe, I didn't know she was going to act like that. I mean, she's supposed to be Michelle's girl."

I laid down on the bed.

Kim crawled up behind me and said, "Don't be mad at me. You know I love you."

I kind of think Kim liked it when I got jealous sometimes, but after sleeping on the couch that night, I don't think this was one of those times.

She said, "Come on, babe, I know you don't think I touched her!"

"I don't know, did you?"

She looked surprised that I said that. She said in disbelief, "Carrie!"

"Kim, I don't know how long she was here! You could have fucked her then played it off when I got home!"

"Babe, I know you don't really believe that!"

"I don't know, should I?"

"You know, Carrie, I was having a really good day until she came over here and caused all these problems. I thought about you all day at work. I have been craving your body all day; I can't believe you let someone stop me from getting my way with you! Didn't you say I can have your body anytime I wanted, however I wanted, and where ever I wanted because you love me and I make you feel so good?"

I said, "Yes!"

"Okay, then! I have wanted to make love to you all day and look what happened. I'm going to have a talk with Michelle. I don't want Angie over here anymore."

"Kim, I don't want that bitch over here anymore either, but you do realize this may cost us our friendship with Michelle?"

"Carrie, I know, but I'm not jeopardizing our relationship for anything or anyone. You had me sleeping on the couch, and I didn't even do anything wrong. Babe, you know I don't like sleeping without you and I don't like it when you're mad at me."

"Are you sure you want to do this, Kim?"

"Did you have me sleeping on the couch?"

"Yes," I said.

"Okay, then! Babe, as long as we've been together, you have never put me on the couch until tonight. I'm not allowing that to happen again! Look, babe, it's me and you in this relationship and I'll never let anyone come between us."

"I know. I'm sorry, Kim. It's just the thought of someone else touching you drives me crazy."

"Yes, I know, babe. So that's it. I'm done with that girl." Then she said, "Baby, come on, don't be mad at me."

She started playing with my breast, asking me to let her make it all better. I just looked at her. When she smiled at me, it melted my heart and I let her have her way with me. I could never resist her.

The next day, Kim called Michelle to see if she could come over by herself to talk. She let her know that she really needed to talk to her alone. She even told her that I wouldn't be there. Michelle agreed to come and that she would be there around eight the next night. That night I made plans with one of my friends that I had met during my freshman year in college. Her name was Katrina, She was straight, had lots of boyfriends, weighed about 145 pounds, and stood about 5'4". She was more or less on the chunky side but very sassy. She was one of those girls who just loved to sleep around. We had planned on going out for just a few drinks, because I had to be at work early the next morning. I was still trying to figure how to get into the writing game, so in the meantime, I took a job as an office production assistant at a small production company.

While we were having drinks, I watched Katrina flirt with guys and get some numbers. A few guys hit on me until they saw the ring on my finger, and of course, one of them was a drunk guy who asked if I liked cheating. I told him no, that I was very much in love. Katrina ended up going home with some guy she knew from school, so I went home. I got home around 10 p.m. Kim was already in bed. I got undressed and crawled into bed with her. I wrapped my arms around her and gave her a kiss on the cheek.

She whispered, "Did you have a good time?"

"Yes, babe, but I missed you. How did everything go tonight?"

"Michelle wasn't happy. I also think once Angie finds out we don't want her over anymore, she will dump Michelle."

"Kim, I wish we could hook Michelle up with someone." As I laid there and thought about it, I said, "What about Vanessa, from the center? Remember we met her a few months ago?"

"Carrie, we have to wait until Michelle gets over Angie, and then hope Vanessa is single. This is a lot to think about and I'm tired. Let's go to sleep."

I was feeling frisky. I said, "Kim?"

She replied, "Yes, babe?"

"I love you."

Kim then pulled me into her arms and said, "I love you more."

I said, "Babe?"

She again said, "Yes, Carrie?"

"How tired are you?"

"Why, babe, do you need me?"

"Yes, but not if you're really tired, Kim."

"Babe, I would really love to make love to you, but I'm really tired."

"Okay, babe. I love you."

She kissed me and we went to sleep. A few days later while we were still in bed and I was trying to get my way with Kim, we heard a knock at the door. Kim got up, but I pulled her back in the bed and said, "Maybe they'll go away." But the person kept knocking. So, I told Kim to get the door. She threw on her pajamas and went to get the door.

Much to her surprise, it was Michelle. She was crying so hard and loud that Kim couldn't understand a word she was saying, and I could hear her all the way from the bedroom. Kim took her over to the couch and sat her down.

I walked out into the living room and said, "What's wrong, Michelle?" I couldn't understand what she was saying either.

Kim said, "Get her some water, Carrie."

I got her the water then sat down next to Kim. After taking a few sips, Michelle began to tell us how Angie broke up with her right after telling her it wouldn't be a good idea for her to come over to our place anymore. She said that Angie wasn't happy and that she said she could come over to our place anytime she wants. "Angie started

yelling, 'You can't tell me what to do!' I said, 'I'm not trying to tell you what to do, Angie, but you're flirting with Kim and all you want to talk about is Kim's mom. They don't want you over there, Angie. Okay I said it! You need to stay away from them!' Angie told me 'If that's the case, I don't need you anymore. Kim is hot, I want her, and what I want I get!'
"

Kim felt so bad. She grabbed my hand and held it when Michelle said that, knowing I was about to storm from the room. Kim did not miss a beat; she just kept talking to Michelle and making sure that I didn't lock myself in the room.

Kim said, "How did she know who my mom was?"

Michelle said, "She looked it up on Google and found out everything about her. She knew you were going to the same school as her, but she said she had no idea how hot you were until she saw you. She said that she read you were a lesbian but didn't know you had a girlfriend."

Kim said, "I'm so sorry, Michelle. You know I would never do anything to hurt you. Nothing happened the other day when she was here, and you know I love Carrie. I don't need or want anyone but her."

I knew that last line was to benefit me, but I was still mad. At the same time, I had to be there for Michelle.

Michelle said, "I know it's not your fault, but I really liked her."

Kim said, "Yeah, but realistically you didn't know who she was, so you liked someone who didn't exist. Why don't you stay with us for a few days? We'll cheer you up. I don't want you to run into her anytime soon. Right, Carrie? We want you here."

"Of course," I said.

Michelle stayed with us for the next four days. Of course I gave Kim hell that night about what Angie said. What she wants, she gets.

Two weeks went by and we were having so much fun with Michelle. It was good to see her smiling again. There were moments when I would see Michelle looking sad, but I would get her attention, to pull her out of her sad thoughts. Michelle went home to get some clothes. She was going to spend the weekend with us.

Kim and I decided to go the farmer's market, where we ran into Vanessa. We decided to invite her over for dinner that night. This time, Kim and I decided to be sneaky while match- making. Michelle met us at our place when we returned. We told her we were going to make a big dinner, drink lots of wine and have a great time. Just as dinner was ready, there was a knock at the door.

Michelle asked, "Are you expecting someone?"

Kim was putting stuff on the table and said, "Yes, can you get that, Michelle?"

Michelle opened the door, and there stood Vanessa.

She said, "Hello, I'm looking for Kim and Carrie." The look on Michelle's face when she saw Vanessa was like, wow!

Vanessa was about 5'7" without her heels and had dark hair and light brown eyes. And talk about someone who had style! I loved the way she dressed. She always looked like she had just stepped right out of a magazine, in the business-sexy section. Vanessa was African American and Italian. She was a very pretty woman. She was a lawyer and had just passed the bar exam three months before.

Laughing because Michelle was just standing at the door with her mouth wide open looking at Vanessa, Kim walked over to the door and said, "Hi, Vanessa, come on in. This is our friend Michelle. You got here just in time; dinner is ready."

Michelle gave Kim that look like she knew she had been set up, but she didn't seem upset. She even had a smile on her face. Vanessa brought a nice Merlot with her and said she didn't want to come empty-handed. It was a great night. We drank wine, talked, and laughed for hours. Finally, Kim and I got up and went into the other room. We could hear Vanessa and Michelle still laughing and talking.

When I woke up the next morning, they were both gone. I wondered how they ended the night and if they'd gone home with each other. Lesbians are known to do that a lot. Kim was in the kitchen making breakfast, so I asked her if she heard them leave the night before.

She said, "Babe, when I got up this morning, they were still here talking but were about to leave. They went out to breakfast. I think we did good, Carrie. I just hope Michelle takes it slow this time."

I walked over to Kim and kissed her. I said, "So, what are we doing today, babe?"

"Well, it's Sunday. I thought we would eat breakfast then spend some time together, all day, just me and you: in bed, on the couch, in the kitchen, and let's not forget the shower."

"You're so bad."

"No, I'm in love with you and I want to physically show you today, all day." Kim teased.

"Can I ask you something? And you have to be totally honest with me." I asked.

"You can ask me anything, babe."

"Do you ever get bored with me?"

"Yes, I'm going to show you how bored I'm with you after we eat."

"Come on, Kim, be honest."

"Carrie, I love you. The day that I get bored with you will be the day I die."

I kissed her and said, "I love you more and more every day!"

"You better, if you don't want me to go crazy. You know I can't live without you."

I just smiled when she said that.

We had just finished with breakfast when Kim got up from her chair and squeezed herself between me and my chair so that she was sitting behind me in my chair. She started kissing my neck slowly then put her hands in my pajama top.

She said, "Oh, I'm so bored," then laughed. She caressed my skin until she reached my breasts, and then started playing with my nipples. Kim knew that was one of my weaker spots. She knew once she started playing with them, she could have her way with me. I loved the way she made me feel. It always felt like it was the first time. She liked trying different things with me. She took my top off and started kissing my back, with the tip of her tongue, up and down the crease of my back. It gave me shivers. Then she turned me around so that I was straddling her, sitting on her lap as she slid her hand into my pajama bottoms. She felt my wetness, and was enjoying playing with my clit, making me feel good. She slid two fingers inside of me, in and out, deeper and deeper. My heart was beating so fast, I literally thought it was going to come out of my chest. Next she pulled me into her. I could feel my body wanting her more and more.

Speaking very slowly, and breathing heavily I said, "Oh, Kim, I want you. Don't stop; this feels so good. I love you, baby."

Kim said, "Have you been a good girl?"

"Oh yes, baby, I've been a very good girl." It felt so good.

She said, "Are you sure, baby?"

"Yes, I'm sure."

"I don't know, Carrie," she said. "You made me sleep on the couch, and I think you should be punished."

"I'm so sorry, baby. Will you forgive me?"

Kim was teasing me when she said, "I don't know, do you think I should, or should I keep punishing you?"

I kept whispering, "Oh baby, this is so good. Don't stop."

She said, "You didn't answer me, Carrie. Should I keep punishing you?"

I was begging! I said, "Yes!" Then it happened. I exploded! It was like heaven. I loved this woman and I just collapsed in her arms. I could not see myself like this with anyone else.

Kim kissed me and said, "I love you." Just as I was catching my breath, she said, "Why don't you go lie down in bed while I do the dishes."

"No, baby," I said, "I'll help you."

She said, "No, you're going to need your rest if I'm going to have my way with you all day."

I said, "Are you sure, babe?"

"Yes, Carrie, trust me on this one. You're mine all day, and we're not answering any doors or the phone today."

I kissed Kim and said, "I love you," as I started to walk to the bedroom. "I'll be waiting for you."

Just as I was falling asleep, I felt Kim crawling under the comforter from the bottom of the bed. Suddenly, her head was between my legs, kissing my thighs. She was licking and sucking on my clitoris. She grabbed my ass with both hands and pulled me closer to her mouth. I couldn't control myself. She had total control of my body. Kim had a way of making my body melt into hers, without effort. I can't emphasize enough just how much I loved the way this woman made love to me; it was like we were one person when I was in her arms. She worked her way up to my breasts and put them into her mouth, like they were juicy grapefruits. She was licking and sucking on both my breasts, going back and forth between them. She began to grind on me. I could feel both our clits rubbing together. Both of us were wet, grinding and feeling so very good. She whispered in my ear, "I'm all yours for life. We'll make love like this forever. I don't want anyone but you. I don't need anyone but you. Tell me you want me forever. Tell me I'm all you need, Carrie."

As I heard her moaning, it was turning me on even more. I said, "I want you, babe."

She whispered, "Tell me you want me forever, Carrie."

I said, "I want you forever." I barely got those words out of my mouth when we both exploded together. There were tears in my eyes.

Kim said, "What's wrong, Carrie? Did I hurt you?"

"No, babe, it was just so beautiful and overwhelming. You and I, I can't see anything else; this is all I want. You're all I need, I know god sent you to me."

She replied, "How did I get so lucky to have you as my best friend, my lover, and the love of my life, Carrie? I'm the lucky one.

You're so loving, caring, and compassionate. I want to make love to all of you." Then Kim said, "Can we talk about something, Carrie?"

I was so far gone with Kim, I said, "Anything you want, baby."

"Carrie, there is something I've wanted to do with you for a long time, but I know you're a virgin. We've been together almost ten years, and I was thinking maybe we could get a strap-on and I could make love to you that way, but if you're not ready for that just tell me, and I'll wait until you are."

All I could say was "Wow! I knew this day would come. I just didn't know when. We have been together since high school and we're now young women, so I think it's time."

She'd waited a long time for this, but I was scared and I didn't want to tell her. After all, I planned on spending the rest of my life with Kim, so I asked myself, why was I so afraid? What was it I was afraid of? I wanted to give all of me to her. I knew she loved me and I loved her.

I sat quietly for a moment and then I heard Kim call my name. "Carrie? Carrie?"

I looked at her and she said, "What are you thinking?"

I didn't say anything.

"What do you think about me making love to you with a strap-on?"

I lied there.

She said, "Okay, I can see you're not ready." When I began to cry, she said, "Oh my God, Carrie, I didn't mean to make you cry, baby, I'm sorry. We don't have to do anything you don't want to do." She started holding me.

I relaxed and began to speak. "Kim, I'm crying because I want to give you all of me. I couldn't love anything or anyone more than I love you. So I think it's time, but I do have to tell you I'm a little scared. Kim, I do want you to make love to me any way you would like. I'm so lost in you. I feel like I was born for you. Sometimes I think I'm going to wake up one day and this would have all been a dream. What did I do to deserve such a wonderful person? What did I do to get this wonderful love from you?"

She surprised me when she said, "I feel the same way, Carrie. I just told myself I was going to stop questioning a good thing and just enjoy. I want to embrace it."

"So you think about that too, Kim? I had no idea."

She said, "Yes, baby, sometimes I wonder since I'm the only person you have been with, do you or will you get curious about being with others. You know, if you want to go out and explore men or more women, and if you do, what would happen to us? I know it would break my heart if you left me, Carrie. I love you so much; I just want you to be happy. So I would have to let you go, even if it meant I would be unhappy for the rest of my life. I just hope that if you ever started to feel that way, you would tell me and not sneak behind my back. That would really hurt me, Carrie. I know we have something special and I would hate to have someone come between us."

Just when we were getting deeper into the conversation, there was knock at the door. I recalled Kim saying we weren't answering any phone calls and no doors today. This was our day alone. We both tried to be quiet until they went away, but the person would not stop knocking. So Kim got up and answered the door. I heard her call my name. "Carrie, your mom is here."

Kim couldn't stand my mother. One night back in high school, Kim crept in my window; she was missing me and wanted to make love. After making love, we fell asleep. My mother knocked at my bedroom door then entered. I quickly threw the covers over Kim so my mom couldn't see her. My mom was drunk and for no good reason, started going off on me. It was the first time Kim saw how my mother treated me. I hadn't done anything wrong. My mom started calling me names, saying I'm just like my father, a loser, and that I would never amount to anything. By the time my mom left my room, I was in tears. Although I was used to her doing that to me, I was embarrassed that Kim had heard everything. Kim never came to my house after that other than to pick me up. She wanted me to move in with her.

Kim came into our room and said, "Put some clothes on; your mother is here."

I was shocked. How did she find out where I lived? Kim and I had moved since we left college. Even still, my mother never once came to see me during my time in college.

"Hello, Mother." She wasn't the hugging type, so I just led her to the living room to have a seat. I said, "How are you? What are you doing here?"

She replied, "Well, Carrie, I'm not doing so good, because I ran into April—you know, Kim's mother—and what she told me is the reason I'm here. What is this I'm hearing about you living in sin with Kim? She told me you two are girlfriends! What the hell is going on with you? Is this true?"

I didn't say anything and Kim went back in the room. I guess she wanted to give Mom and I some privacy.

Mom said, "Answer me right now, Carrie!"

"Mom, I tried to tell you last time I came home, but you wouldn't make time for me. I asked you over and over again, but you were too busy with your boyfriend. I love her, Mom."

She said, "Pack your shit; you're going home *now*!"

"But, Mom, I love her!"

She said, "Did you hear what I said, Carrie?"

"Yes, but Mom, I want to be with her." Then it hit me. I was grown and I could live how I wanted. I was already home. "No, Mom, I'm not leaving. This is where I live and who I love and that's not going to change!" All I could think is how dare she come down here and tell me I'm living in sin and to pack my stuff to leave with her. What did she mean I was living in sin? She never once took me to church, so what did she know about living in sin? As far back as I remembered, my mom never cared about me. When I was growing up, all I was to my mom was a reminder of how much she hated my father, who I never even met. Every time she got mad at me she would say, "You're like your father," and when she would make me cry she would say to me, "Stop crying, you look just like your ugly father." So, I would go in my room and yell at God for making me look like my dad and for making my mom hate me so much. She was the kind of mom who didn't care what I did, as long as it didn't bother her. She always had a new boyfriend who she gave all of her attention to. So how could she come down here to get me? What was she going to do with me, make me stay in my room like a little kid, while she played with her new boyfriends for the rest of her life? I guess it didn't matter since I had no plans to live with her anyway.

She said, "I'm not going to tell you again to pack your stuff. Let's go now!"

"No, Mom, I'm not going anywhere! I'm grown; this is where I live and how I live. I'm home!"

She said, "Okay, if you want to stay here, know this: I'm cutting you off! I don't want anything to do with you as long as you're living in sin. Don't call me, don't write me, and don't even think about e-mailing me. You are dead to me!"

Then she stormed out and slammed the door. I just broke down and started crying. I fell to my knees. Kim came in and picked me up.

She said, "Come on, baby. It's going to be okay." Then she laid me down on the bed, crawled under the covers with me, and held me until I cried myself to sleep. When I woke up hours later with swollen eyes, I wondered what I was going to do now as far as family went. I didn't know my father, my grandfather had died before I was born, and my grandmother wasn't in my life because my mother had cut her out of my life. I didn't even know where she lived. I also didn't have any aunts or uncles because my mom was like me, an only child. So now I had no blood family in my life. What would happen to me if Kim and I didn't make it as a couple? This was the reality of my life. I was so scared. I didn't know what to do, so I just lied there in Kim's arms and cried.

I was upset and depressed for the next few weeks. Kim tried her best to cheer me up. But I was just so hurt. I couldn't see past not having any family in my life. Sometimes I wondered why God put me with my mother, when he knew she wouldn't love me, but they say you're not supposed to question God.

As time went by, I got better. I knew I was on my own, from that point on. Kim assured me that she would never leave me and that her and her mother would always be my family. She also told me my mom would come around in time. With that said, I kept my hopes up. I just hung on to Kim and her mom as my family, waiting for my mom to come around.

Chapter Eight

She's Back and Things Aren't

Always as They Seem

Kim was a counselor for young gay groups and it was her weekend to go to camp with the kids. She had to do this once a month. I would drop her off at the center whenever she had to go. They would go up on Friday and the volunteers would go up on Saturdays for the activities. Kim always called me when she got there Friday night and then during breakfast Saturday morning. It was Friday, and on schedule, Kim called me that night. We talked for a while then she sang me to sleep because she knew I couldn't sleep that well without her.

The next morning during breakfast when she called me, she said that she had to tell me something and that I was going to have to trust her. Of course, this made me nervous. She said, "Babe, can you do this for me?"

Just as she said this, I heard Angie in the background say, "Hi, Carrie, it's me, Angie. Don't worry. I'm going to take good care of Kim."

I yelled, "Oh my God! Kim, you didn't!" then I hung up the phone. I sat there, numb. What was she doing with Angie? Oh my God, she was fucking Angie! My heart was aching. I was in a daze and I needed to leave. I wasn't sticking around for this. I packed my shit, but didn't know where to go. I went online and looked up hotels. Once I found one, I headed out. While this was happening, my phone kept ringing. It was Kim calling me over and over. I wasn't about to answer and listen to her bullshit. She must have been fucking Angie this whole time behind my back. She would not stop calling so I turned my phone off. Once I got into my hotel room, I sat down and that's when it all hit me. I started crying. How could she do this to me? I thought she loved me. She said I was all she needed. How could she look me in my eyes this whole time and then do this behind my back? My heart was broken. I felt so betrayed, as if my life with Kim was a lie. Then it hit me again. I had no one; I was now on my own. I cried myself to sleep in that lonely hotel room.

When I woke up the next morning, I lied there not knowing what I was going to do. I felt so empty inside, but at the same time I felt all of the pain in my heart. All those years with Kim and now it was over. I wanted to die. All I could think was why? Was I not meant to be loved? Was this supposed to be part of my life's plan? It hurt so bad thinking about Kim with someone else. I was so deep in thought my hotel phone startled me when it rang. They wanted to know if I was going to stay another night. I told them yes, since I had nowhere else to go. I lied in bed and cried all day. I knew a lot of girls were always after Kim, but why would she choose to cheat on me or even leave me for Angie, of all people? She was such a loser, but I guess Kim finally gave in to temptation. I didn't get it. Kim had been bugging me to marry her and we had planned on that being the night she took my virginity, our wedding night. She kept saying we were going to live the rest of our lives together; this was something we always talked about. She said she would never leave me or cheat on me, and now look at what she has done!

I knew I couldn't live any longer. I got out of the bed, drove to the nearest drugstore and got some pills. My plan was to take as many pills as I could until I died. I had nothing to live for anymore. I had no mother, no Kim, and no family whatsoever. I had spent my childhood alone and I didn't want to go back to that, along with a broken heart. After getting the strongest over-the-counter sleeping pills I could find, I drove back to the hotel, parked my car, and walked through the lobby looking a mess. When I got to the elevators, I heard someone call my name. I turned around and Kim, Michelle, and April were in the lobby. Kim was coming at me so fast I kept pushing the elevator button. I needed to get away.

When Kim got to me, I pushed her away and said, "Get away from me! I hate you!" She looked at me when I said that, tears filling her eyes.

She said, "Please don't say that, Carrie."

Then Michelle chimed in, "Carrie, you need to listen to Kim, please!"

The elevator doors opened and I jumped in.

Kim jumped in and said, "I'm coming with you."

I yelled, "Get out!"

At this point people in the hotel were watching us. You could hear people whispering, "Isn't that April Springs?"

April said, "Kim, get off the elevator. I'm going to talk to her."

Kim replied, "But Mom . . ."

April said, "Kim, you wait down here while I go talk to her, if that's okay, Carrie?"

I had to say yes. I couldn't say no to April. She was always so sweet to me. So, I said, "Okay." When we got to my room, I asked what she was doing here.

She said, "I wanted to make sure my girl was okay."

I couldn't believe she was calling me her girl, as if she really cared what happened to me. This was something new to me. The only person who ever cared about me was Kim, but I knew that was gone.

She said, "When Kim called me in a panic and told me that you disappeared, I had to find you."

"But how did you find me?"

"You paid for the room with your credit card."

I said, "Oh. I don't ever want to talk to Kim ever again. I'm done with her. I'm done with everything." I started crying.

April said, "Don't say that, sweetheart. I don't ever want to hear you say that." Then she hugged me.

I said, "You don't understand. I have nothing now. If I don't have Kim, I don't have anything. Kim was my family."

She said, "I'm your family, sweetheart, and believe it or not, Kim and Michelle are your family." She wiped my eyes and then said, "I want to talk to you. I really need you to listen to me and hear me out."

I said, "Okay, I can do that."

"You know I would never lie to you, right, Carrie?"

"Yes."

"Kim did nothing wrong."

I interrupted her and then said, "But Kim was with Angie. She's cheating on me! She broke my heart."

"Carrie, Kim never cheated on you. She loves you too much. She calls me all the time and tells me how much she loves you, and that she can't wait to marry you. She always sounds happy when she's with you. Kim told me what happened, and this girl Angie sounds like bad news. Kim loves you so much that she had Michelle get her from camp and bring her home. Her boss told her if she left, she would be fired. What do you think Kim did?"

I said, "But why was she there with Angie in the first place?" Listening to April, I began to feel a little better.

"Kim told me she didn't know that Angie had volunteered. When she got to breakfast and saw Angie, she called you right away. When she tried to tell you about it, Angie walked by and yelled something in the background. Kim said when you heard that, you immediately hung up and would not answer your phone. Now, from what I understand you have been having problems with this Angie, because she's after Kim. You need to understand that doesn't mean Kim wants her."

I didn't say anything, I sat there listening.

Then she said, "Sweetheart, do you love Kim?"

I said, "You know I do, very much."

She said, "Do you think Kim loves you?"

I said in my sad voice, "I don't know anymore."

"Carrie, think about it; is she always there when you need her?"

"Yes."

"Does she tell you she loves you?"

Again I said, "Yes."

She asked, "Sometimes or all the time?"

I said, "All the time?" like I wasn't sure.

She said, "Come on, Carrie."

"Okay, all the time."

"Do you really think if she didn't love you and was cheating on you, she would be going through all of this? I mean, she picked you over her job. And you know how much Kim loves that job."

I said, "I guess."

Then she said something that made feel better. "You know, I remember when Kim was first falling in love with you. It was during high school. When she would come home from school and you weren't with her, all she wanted to do was talk about you. The look in her eyes told me she was head over heels for you. I said to myself, *My baby is in love; I hope she doesn't get hurt.* However, when I saw you two interact I knew you both were in love. You know, she still has that look in her eyes when you two are together. But when I got here and looked in my baby's eyes, all I saw was hurt. Do you want to hurt Kim?"

I said, "No, never."

"That's what you're doing every time you don't trust Kim. Carrie, I know it's hard for you to trust people, but my baby has never hurt you, and I don't think she ever will. You and Kim have something very special and people will always be envious of that and try to come between the two of you. But you're going to have to be strong and not let that happen. Now, do you really believe that Kim cheated on you?"

"No, not anymore."

She said, "Okay, sweetheart, you're going to have to start trusting Kim at some point. You can't always run every time you think something is wrong. You need to talk it out with her."

"I know, but before I met you and Kim, I didn't know what it was like to have someone actually love me. Sometimes I think I'm waiting for it to all fall apart."

"You can't think that way, Carrie. What you need to do is love Kim and let Kim love you. Now, if someone tries to come between you two, then you're going to have to fight for that love. I know it's going to be hard sometimes, but if you truly love Kim, you'll fight for her love. As you can see, she's doing that by having all of us involved with finding you."

"I never thought about it that way, and I guess you're right."

"Okay, can Kim come up here and talk to you now? You know Kim is losing her mind down there; she's crazy about you and needs to know you still want to be with her."

"Yes, she can come up."

"Okay, Carrie, but before I go, I want you to make me a promise."

"Okay."

"Next time you feel upset and want to run, will you promise to call me first?"

I said, "Okay."

Then she said, "No, promise me."

"Okay, I promise."

"Okay, I'm going downstairs and I'll send Kim up, but one last thing before I go. I need you to give me that bag you brought up."

I said, "What bag?"

"Carrie, I know whatever is in that bag isn't good for you."

I handed her the bag, she hugged me and kissed me on the cheek, then said, "I love you."

I said, "I love you, too."

A few minutes later, I heard a knock at my door. It was Kim. When I opened the door, Kim grabbed me and hugged me so tightly. She started saying, "Carrie, I'm so sorry. I didn't know she was going to be there."

"No, baby, it's my fault. I should have trusted you. I know you love me. I just heard her voice in the background and went crazy. I'm the one who's sorry, Kim. I don't hate you. I love you. Babe, I'm sorry that you lost your job. I know how much you love that job. Why do you even put up with me? Why, Kim? Can't you see I'm no good? My own mother doesn't love me, so why do you?" I felt bad that Kim lost her job because of me. I was crying at this point.

She said, "Babe, don't you know that you're the best thing that ever happened to me? I love you because you're beautiful inside and out. You're smart, funny, and most importantly, you fill my heart with happiness." Then she held my face with both hands and said, "Babe, yes, I loved that job, but not as much as I love you!"

"Kim, I'm really going to try hard to trust you. Your mom told me something and it makes sense to me—why I'm the way I'm about trusting you. Babe, I promise I'll do my best to trust you. Will you forgive me?"

"You know I will, Carrie. I love you; I want you to be happy."

I felt relieved and said, "Kim, I love you so much. I'm really sorry."

"I love you, too. I've been looking for you for two days and thought I lost you forever. Thank God my mother knew how to find you. Please don't ever run away again; you scared me. Carrie, how do you expect me to live without my beautiful wife?"

"I'm sorry. Next time I'll talk it out with you, I promise." I looked at her and said, "Babe, what are you going to do about a job?"

"We won't worry about that right now. I just want you to come home. Are you ready to come home?"

I looked at her and she said, "Now what? Babe, you're wearing me out."

I said, "Well, I did pay for the night. I'm thinking we could stay here tonight and let me make everything up to you!"

She kissed me and said, "Okay, let me go downstairs and tell my mother and Michelle that everything is okay so they can leave. I'll be back in a few minutes."

I replied, "Okay, babe. When you get back, I'll show you how much I love you and how sorry I am."

After that, I did my best to trust Kim. One night at a party, I was so proud of myself. This girl kept hitting on Kim whenever I would walk around and talk to people. Even though I could see what was going on, I didn't get upset. I heard Kim tell the girl that she was married, but the girl didn't seem to care. She was a little buzzed from drinking, so Kim finally waved me over to her and said, "This is my wife of almost ten years, and for life. So, no thank you."

I kissed Kim and said, "I love you." The girl walked off with an attitude.

Kim said, "I'm so proud of you and I love you even more."

I even started playing games with Kim. When Kim and I went out, we frequented the same places most of the time. Everybody knew I was her girl and left us alone. But when Kim and Michelle showed up at the bar without me, I was told that girls send drinks over to Kim, even though they knew she had a girlfriend. Women can be so shady at times.

Kim either sent the drinks back or gave them to Michelle.

Well, one night while Kim was out at the bar with Michelle, I came in and sat in a corner so Kim and Michelle didn't see me.

I watched Kim send a few drinks back, and that's when I decided to send her a drink. I sent a message along with it.

I told the waitress to let her know that I thought she was really hot and that I had a hotel room around the corner. If she wanted to meet me there, she needed to accept this drink.

A few minutes later, the waitress came back with the drink and said, "The young lady said 'thank you, but no thank you!'"

Kim never even turned around to see who sent her the drink.

So I sent the drink back with another message that said, "I think you really want this drink."

But the waitress came back again and said, "She said to tell you she is very happily married."

I then handed the waitress the key to my hotel room and a twenty-dollar bill for her troubles and said, "Hand her this room key, then tell her that Carrie loves her and needs to feel her body against her right now." I saw Kim turn around to look at me when the waitress pointed me out.

Kim came over and said, "Baby, you're so bad!" We had a great time in the hotel that night.

Our ten-year anniversary was coming and I wanted to do something special with Kim. She wasn't very happy at her new job as a school administrator. I felt really bad about it and wanted her to at least have a good anniversary. We were going to go to Vermont and get married. But Kim could not get the time off since she had just started the job. So instead, I made reservations at Hotel Del Coronado. It was a famous hotel; they had shot the movie *Some Like It Hot* there, the classic movie with Marilyn Monroe, Tony Curtis, and Jack Lemon. Kim loved that hotel. My plan was to take her to one of the restaurants downstairs. I also got the honeymoon suite for us. I got some whipped cream and chocolate just in case she was in a kinky mood. I got lots of candles and planned to set them all around the room. The plan was for us to go for a walk on the beach right after we were done with dinner. When we got back to the lobby, I was going to pretend I had to go to the bathroom, then run up to the room and light all of the candles. I was trying to do all the things I thought she would love. Kim had shown me all through the years how much she loved me and it was long overdue that I showed her how much I loved her and knew how lucky I was to have her. I would have rose petals all over the bed, and in the middle of the bed with a big cake that said, "Happy 10th Anniversary."

Kim came home from work the night of our anniversary and didn't remember it was our special day. But, it was okay. She wasn't very happy, so I told her to get dressed, that I would be taking her out to dinner. She sat down on the couch and said, "Babe, I'm too tired."

"Come on, babe, tomorrow is Saturday. You can sleep in, I promise." She took a shower to wake up and then she put on the clothes I had laid out for her. She looked so pretty, like she always did. Right before we got on the freeway, I made her put on the blindfold I had waiting in the car for her. We went over the bridge that went to Coronado. When we pulled up to the hotel, I told her to take the blindfold off. She looked around and said, "Oh, babe, my favorite hotel!"

I said, "Yes, we're having dinner here."

She loved it. After dinner, we went for a walk on the beach like we used to back in college. We held hands and talked.

"Babe, I'm sorry you're so unhappy at your job, and I know it's my fault. I wanted to make this night good for you." I said.

"Babe, like I said before, it's okay. I would rather have you then that job." Kim admitted.

When we got back to the lobby, I told her I needed to use the restroom before we departed. I ran to the room and called down to room service, asking them to bring the cake up quickly. I lit all the candles around the room, but not on the cake. The last thing I wanted to do was start a fire! When the cake got there, I ran back down and got Kim. I said, "I'm sorry, babe, I got a phone call from work. Are you ready to go?"

She said, "Yes."

"Okay, Kim, put your blindfold back on."

She said, "There's more?"

"Yes, babe, this is a very special night for us." I grabbed her hand and led her to the room. Once we got inside the room, I took her blindfold off and said, "Happy Anniversary."

She saw the cake on the bed and said, "Oh my God! I'm so sorry, babe, I forgot." She felt so bad.

But I said, "No, you didn't."

She said, "I'm really sorry, babe, but I did."

I took her hand and said, "Babe, no you didn't. Every time you told me you loved me, you didn't forget. Every single day when you treated me with love, you didn't forget. Every time you were there when I needed you, you didn't forget. Every time you made love to me, you didn't forget. Every time you held me when I was sad, you didn't forget. Every time you looked in my eyes and told me you would love me forever, you didn't forget. It was me who needed to remember, and so I did. I love you, Kim. Thank you for a wonderful ten years."

She had tears in her eyes and said, "I have no words. How do I top that? All I can say is I love you, Carrie. You are my heart and you're about to become my wife. I can't ask for anything more."

I put on the song "Baby I Love Your Way" by Peter Frampton and said, "Dance with me." I spent that night in Kim's arms while she slept. For the rest of the weekend, we didn't come out of our room. We made love until checkout time.

Chapter Nine

Whoever Said You Can Go Home

Again Lied

Six months had passed and Christmas was coming. I didn't know what we were doing and so I asked Kim if she was going home for Christmas. By then, we were close to our eleventh year together and I had become even closer to Kim's mom. She told me she had spoken to her mother and yes, her mother told us to come home for Christmas.

I said, "Kim, you know I can't go home for Christmas. My mom wants nothing to do with me anymore, so I'll stay here and wait for you to come home."

Kim said, "No, silly, we're both going home to my mom's house. I talked to her about what happened. She said you are now her daughter and you have to come home for Christmas. She also wants to talk to you. She feels bad about telling your mother about us. She had no idea that your mother didn't know after all these years."

Four days before Christmas, we headed to L.A. It was nice when we drove up to the house. It was all decorated with lots of Christmas lights, snowmen, and reindeers. It was so pretty.

Kim said, "I see she went all out again. We really need to give her some grandbabies."

When we walked in the house, Kim's mom was standing in the foyer. She grabbed Kim and hugged her, "I have missed you so much."

Although Kim always talked to her mom on the phone, it had been about seven months since she had last seen her. Every time I saw them embrace, I always wished it were me who had a mother that gave me affection and loved me the way Kim's mom loved her.

Kim said, "Mom, what's with all the decorations? I'm grown now."

Her mom said, "I know, Kim. I miss having my little girl around. So I thought maybe you and Carrie could humor me and pretend to like it."

I said, "I love it. I've never had a Christmas with decorations like this. It's beautiful."

April hugged me and said, "Thank you. I missed seeing your face around here too!" Then she grabbed my hand and said, "I want to talk to you." She told Kim we would be back in a few minutes and to go put our stuff away.

We went to her office, which had a very large desk with a computer and a bunch of pictures of Kim. On the wall, there were pictures of April on the set of the sitcom she was famous for as a teenager.

"Carrie, I just wanted to say I'm so sorry. I had no idea that your mother didn't know. I thought you told her. When I ran into her at the store and mentioned how good you two were doing and how happy you both were out in San Diego, I thought she knew. I would never do anything to hurt you. Give your mom some time; she will come around." April explained.

"But it's been a while."

"I know, sweetheart, but time will tell. In the meantime, you can always come here. This is also your home now. If you need anything, I want you to call me. I don't care what it is. If I can't do it, I'll get someone who can. Do you understand?"

And with a smile on my face I said, "Yes, ma'am."

"That's another thing; I want you to call me Mom. After all, you are marrying my baby." April ordered with love in her eyes.

That night, I slept with Kim in her bed and we held each other. For the first time in my life, I felt loved and safe, like I had a real family. The next day we woke up to the smell of breakfast. When we went down to the kitchen, Rosa had made all of Kim's favorite foods. It was all so good. Kim's mom came down and said, "After you two finish eating, get dressed. We're going Christmas shopping."

With so many presents already under the tree, I guessed we needed more. The tree was about twelve feet tall and it was so beautiful. It had what I think was white spray on it to make it look like it was covered in snow. It had silver and gold bulbs, and pretty little bulbs of all colors—red, blue, green, and yellow. I knew I was a grown woman now, but I couldn't help feeling like a little girl making up for lost time, for all the Christmas holidays that I didn't have while growing up.

We were having so much fun shopping. Kim asked me to go and find her mother. She said she needed to buy something and she didn't want me to see what it was. So I went to find April. As I walked through the mall, I spotted a hat in one of the windows that I knew my mother would love. It made me sad to think I wouldn't be seeing her for Christmas, even if we never had a Christmas. Mom loved hats so I decided to go in and buy it for her. Most people would say to forget my mom after everything she had done to me, but all I wanted was my mother's love. It wasn't that easy for me to give up. I had this need inside of me to have her love.

After I bought the hat, I was off to find Kim's mom. With no sign of her, I decided to find something special for Kim. I wanted to get us rings, even though Kim had gotten me a ring some years back. I wanted us to have matching wedding bands. I picked out sterling silver bands for us, and then I got Kim a silver necklace with her name on it. I was also trying to figure out what to get Kim's mom.

I knew it had to be something special; April was a special woman and though she was gone a lot while Kim was growing up, she always seemed to support Kim in any way she could. She even took me in when my mother disowned me. I couldn't think of anything, so I went to find Kim and ask her what kind of things her mother liked. I found her in the food court, talking to her mother. When she saw me she said, "Where have you been, Carrie? I've been looking for you and calling your cell phone. I thought you went to find Mom."

"I went to look for her, but then I got distracted by something I saw in a store window. So I went in to buy it. Kim, I need to talk to you alone for a minute."

Kim said, "Okay. Mom we'll be right back."

We walked a few feet away from the food court, and I said, "Kim, I really want to get your mother something special, but I have no idea what she likes."

Kim said, "That's easy; just get anything that has to do with her face." Then she laughed.

I laughed and said, "What does that mean, Kim? Wait! Oh my gosh, Kim, I just got an idea. Do you have any pictures of your mom and yourself together?"

She said, "Sure, lots of them. Why?"

I had seen this store while I was walking around that could take your picture and make it look like an oil painting in two days. Although it was kind of cheesy, I thought she would like it because it would be her and her daughter, who she loved so much.

I said, "Okay, great, Kim! Can I borrow one when we get back to your house?"

"Yes, you can borrow one. Carrie, it's your house, too. Remember what my mom said?"

"Yes, Kim, I'm sorry."

She said, "Why do you want a picture, Carrie?"

"Just trust me, and don't ask, okay?"

"Okay, babe."

When we walked back to Kim's mom, a few people were getting her autograph, so we smiled and waited, and then we headed home. When we got there, I went into the guest room to wrap my presents, while Kim went into her room to wrap hers. About an hour later, Kim's mom called us down for dinner. As we were eating, I brought up the subject of my mother. April asked me if I'd called her since I'd been there.

"No, but I did get her a Christmas gift, and I would like to take it to her on Christmas Day." Kim said, "Okay, I'll take you."

"I would like to go by myself, if that's okay?"

Kim said, "Okay. Are you sure?"

"Yes, I'm sure."

That night while lying in bed, Kim said, "Get up. Let's go downstairs while Mom is sleeping."

We headed to the family room. Kim put on the song "The Way You Look Tonight." We were dancing cheek to cheek when halfway through the song, we looked up and saw April standing there watching us.

"How can something so beautiful be illegal to do? I don't understand why someone would not want you two married. It's so very clear that you two are very much in love." April said proudly.

Kim said, "I'm sorry, Mom. Did we wake you up?"

"No, sweetheart, I was getting some water. I saw you two and couldn't help watching something so special." She then walked over to us and kissed me on the cheek. "Thank you for keeping my daughter so happy."

When she headed upstairs I said, "I love your mom." The next day I took the picture that Kim had given me of her mom and herself to the mall. The store clerk said I could pick it up in two days. After I picked it up, I took it to be gift-wrapped.

Christmas Day came. Kim loved our wedding bands and was so excited about her necklace. Kim and her mom bought me so much stuff: clothes, jewelry, and really cute shoes. But I think my favorite was a license plate to put on Kim's car that said, Carrie's Girl."

Kim's mom was sitting by the tree when I said to her, "Don't move, I have something special for you." I ran up to the guest room where I had hidden the picture of her and Kim. I came downstairs, handed it to her, and said, "I hope you like it."

When April opened it, tears filled her eyes.

"How did you know this is my favorite picture of Kim and me?" She got up hugged me and said, "Thank you so much. You're now my favorite daughter-in-law!"

Kim said, "Mom, she's your only daughter-in-law."

I said, "I better be!" as I tapped Kim on the hand. We laughed, opened the rest of our presents, and then had breakfast.

After breakfast, I got dressed and decided it was time to go and see my mother. As I drove, I was kind of scared. I didn't know if she would talk to me, or even accept the present I had gotten her. Would she even open the door and would she call me a sinner again? Lost in my thoughts, I finally realized I had pulled up to my mom's house. It took me a few minutes to get out of the car. I took a deep breath and got out. As I walked to the door, I could feel my heart beating rapidly. I stopped at the front door and took another deep breath, then knocked with my heart still beating at what seemed like five hundred miles per hour, but there was no answer. So, I knocked again, and still there was no answer. I walked to the side window to see if I could see Mom inside. When I looked through the window, not only was she not there, but everything inside the house was gone.

I went to the neighbor's house to see if she knew where my mom was or where she had moved to. Ms. Gray was about seventy years old and lived alone, but it never stopped her from being nosey. I knew she was the right neighbor to ask. When I knocked at her door, she had been standing in the window watching me like she always did when someone would come to the neighborhood. When she opened her door, she asked if she could help me, as if she had never seen me before. She always did that, thinking we didn't see her in the window all the time.

"Hello, Ms. Gray. I'm Carrie, you know, the daughter of the woman who has been living next door to you for years?" I explained.

She said, "Oh, yes, how are you?"

"I'm okay, I was looking for my mother; do you know where she moved to?"

She said, "No, honey, all I know is a big moving truck pulled up about two months ago and I haven't seen her since."

"Ms. Gray do you know if she left a forwarding address?"

"No, she didn't come over, I'm sorry. I have to go. My game show is coming on now; you take care."

I walked to the car and sat there. Where was my mother? Had she really cut me out of her life? I had figured she needed some time to process everything, and in time she would come around. I began to cry. What was I going to do? I decided to call her cell phone. It rang once and then it picked up and the message said the phone was disconnected. My heart dropped. I began to cry again. Then I got angry. All of my life, my mom had treated me like she didn't want me. Now she had gotten her way. I was out of her life, with no sign of her anywhere and no way to contact her. I felt so alone, as if I had no one. I sat thinking about the only woman who had ever loved me—Kim. I drove back to her house, hugged her, and cried.

She said, "Carrie, what's wrong?"

Crying, I said, "I have no mom and no family."

Kim responded, "What happened, babe? Did she tell you to go away and not come back?"

I said, "No, Kim. She was gone."

"What do you mean? She wasn't home?"

"No, she moved without any forward address and her cell phone is disconnected."

Kim said, "Carrie, I'm so sorry. I'm here for you, babe, and you were wrong when you said you don't have any family. We are your family and always will be." I cried and hugged Kim so tight, I think I might even have been hurting her.

Kim's mom came in and said, "What's wrong?"

Kim told her what happened.

April said, "Awe, sweetheart, I'm so sorry. I know it's not the same to you, but we're here for you; no matter what."

Although I knew I had Kim and her mother, it still hurt that my mom had packed up and left. How could someone do that to her own child? I started crying more and said, "Kim, why doesn't she love me?"

Kim didn't know what to say. She held me. I cried all night, thinking about what had happened.

Chapter Ten

I Will Never Be the Same

After that, things had changed with me. I became more distant toward everyone. Even though I knew Kim loved me so much, I was still so numb inside that, no matter how hard Kim tried, she could not feel the love that I had for her. I began drinking more and more every day. She didn't really like that; I started staying out all night, sometimes not coming home for days. I started missing work so often that I got fired. I didn't tell Kim. So when the notice came that my car payments were three months behind and they were going to repo my car, Kim said we needed to talk.

I said, "Okay, do you want to leave me like my mother did?"

She felt so bad, but said, "It's not me who is leaving you. It's you who left me the day your mother left you. I have been patient. I have waited up night after night, wondering if you were coming home. I don't know who you have been with, or if you're safe. I pray every night that you come home safe and come back to me. Carrie, I can't do this anymore. You're not only killing yourself, but you're breaking my heart. You're pushing me away from you; I don't know what to do anymore. I can't sit and watch you kill yourself anymore. It's killing me inside. Can't you see that? Do you think this is really solving anything?"

I didn't say anything. I only sat there, thinking about everything I could remember I did while staying out all night getting drunk. I felt really bad. I didn't want to sober up, because I would have to deal with all of my demons. You see, I hadn't been only getting drunk; I had done the unspeakable. Yes, I cheated, and more than a few times. I didn't want to tell Kim; it would kill her, and I didn't want to hurt her. Everything had changed. The way I was treating Kim—not coming home at night and now sleeping with others—all the innocence of our relationship was gone. But there was something even worse. Not only had I slept with someone else, but the first time was with a guy, and more than one. The first guy had taken my virginity, something Kim had waited years to do.

Although I had been drinking, I remembered it so clearly. It was me, Katrina, and some other people I had met at the bar. The bar was closing and they suggested we take the party back to this guy Billy's place. When we walked into his apartment, it looked like the typical bachelor's place. He had a bar back in the corner with beer cans stacked high on top of it, a couch covered with blankets to cover up what were probably holes, a big flat-screen TV mounted on the wall, and clothes all over the place. Billy began to pick up his clothes off the couch and told us to have a seat. All five of us could not fit on the couch, so I sat on the barstool, knocking over some of the cans.

"Oops, I'm sorry," I said. I was tipsy at that point.

Billy said, "You have to take a shot now! Anyone who knocks over the cans always has to take a shot."

So I did, and three shots later, I found myself making out with Billy.

It was like I forgot I had a girlfriend at home. Once I got drunk, the reality of my life went out the window. He started to feel me up through my blouse, and I said, "Not here; not in front of everyone," so he led me to his room. He took my blouse off and began to grind on me. I was drunk at this point, so I guess I was into it. Then he took his pants off. He had no underwear on, so I could see his hard erection. Then he began to take my pants off. I let him. It was like I was watching myself do this, and I could not stop it. Then he reached into his side drawer and pulled out a condom, slipped it on, and began to enter me. Although I was drunk, I could feel the pain of him entering me for the first time. It was all over in about three minutes. He was so drunk I guess that's all he could endure. It was bad. Kim had waited for all of those years and I just gave it up in three minutes. I knew she would never forgive me.

The next time it happened, I was getting drunk with my friend Katrina at her house. She had a little money and a nice condo. Some friends were over and she had told me earlier I could sleep in the guest room. She knew I was getting too drunk to drive. This really cute guy kept flirting with me. I found myself making out with him on the couch. He asked me if I could show him to the bathroom. When we got to the door, he pulled me in with him. He backed me up against the wall and pulled out his big penis. He pulled my leg up and entered me. He was going at it, and then he bent me over the sink and took me doggie style. The worst was after he came, I noticed he didn't have a condom on. What was I doing? I passed out and found myself in Katrina's guest room the next morning, but I remembered what had happened. I told myself I was going to get AIDS, but I kept putting off getting tested.

Lately, I had not been feeling well. I was thinking while Kim sat there, telling me she was putting her foot down and did not want to deal with this anymore, that I was going to get a test done tomorrow. Then I heard, "Carrie, are you even listening to me?"

"Yes, I'm sorry, I need to lie down. I don't feel well."

She said, "Fine, Carrie, why don't you go take a shower and then take a nap. We'll talk when you wake up."

I got in the shower and thought about Kim. What I had done to her and how would I tell her? I knew if I did, I would lose her forever. I really loved her and I didn't want that to happen. I was too afraid to tell her. How would she react? What would she do?

I began to shake in the shower. I sat down and let the water run all over me. I must have been crying loud because Kim came in and said, "What's going on? Come on, Carrie, get up. Let's get you out of the shower."

She grabbed a towel and dried me off.

While I was crying, I kept repeating, "I'm sorry, I'm sorry," over and over again.

Kim put my pajamas on me then laid me in the bed. She said, "Go to sleep, we'll talk when you wake up."

I lied there thinking about Kim until I fell asleep. When I woke up hours later, my head hurt so badly that I could not get up. How could I have betrayed the woman I love, the woman who had shown me nothing but love since the day I met her? How could I hurt the woman I loved so much this way? How could I treat her so badly? My mom had done a number on me. It made me lose everything I ever loved. I knew I had to tell Kim.

Deep down inside, I knew she would leave me, but I could not keep my secrets anymore. How do you tell the woman that you love that you have betrayed her? How do you tell the only person who loves you and has cherished you since the day she met you that you have done everything that you promised not to do? How could I look her in the eyes and hurt her like that? My eyes filled with tears just as Kim walked in the room.

She said, "Hey, how are you feeling, Carrie?"

"My head hurts."

"I'll get you something to take." When Kim came back into the room, she handed me some pills and a glass of water. I took them and then she asked, "Are you hungry?"

"No, I feel nauseated."

"Well, you need to eat something, then. I'll make you some soup and get you some crackers; that should help." She walked out of the room.

I was so scared. I knew she wanted to talk tonight and I was wondering what she was thinking. It seemed like she was trying to get me sober and clear enough to talk. I knew it was going to be a long night. I could hear voices coming from the living room, but I didn't hear anyone knock at the door. Whoever it was must have come while I was sleeping. I assumed it was Michelle. Twenty minutes later, Kim came in with soup and crackers. She said, "After you eat this, I would like you to come into the living room so we can talk."

All I could say is, "Okay." But I was scared as hell. I couldn't finish my soup because my stomach was doing somersaults. I got up, brushed my teeth, washed my face, grabbed the bowl, and walked out of the room heading toward the living room. When I saw who was in there with Kim, I dropped my bowl and it splattered all over the floor.

Billy said, "Hi, Carrie," as he started to get the broken pieces of the bowl off of the floor. "How have you been? I've been trying to track you down for weeks. I had such a good time with you that night that I wanted to get to know you better. I found out where you live from your friend Katrina."

My heart dropped. I looked at Kim; she had tears coming down her face. She looked so hurt, and tears filled my eyes. Then she spoke.

Kim said, "Billy is here because he would like to take you out on a real date. He said ever since he spent that special night with you, he can't get you out of his mind. I'm going to my room so that you guys can make your plans."

Kim headed to our room, which she was now calling her room. I told Billy I could not talk right now and that he had to go! He kept asking for my number and I started pushing him out the door. I told him he's not getting my number and that I could not see him anymore. Then I closed the door behind him.

Very quickly, I walked back to the room. When I opened the bedroom door, Kim was packing her stuff. I didn't know what to say, so I just yelled out. "Don't leave me! I love you. I'm sorry. Please, Kim. I didn't mean to hurt you. I'm sorry, baby. Please, Kim, I'm begging you; don't leave me. I'll do anything. Please!" I was bawling my eyes out, begging, and pleading for Kim not to leave me.

Kim wasn't saying a word, until I said, "Kim, please, don't do this to us." Why did I say that?

She turned around, looked at me, and said very loudly, "What did you just say?"

I said, "Please don't leave me."

"No, you said, 'Don't do this to us'! Is that what I heard you say, Carrie? Answer me, Carrie, right now!"

I had never seen or heard Kim so mad since the day I met her. "All I meant was don't leave me, Kim." I was so nervous at this point. Then she started letting me have it.

"Carrie, you left me a long time ago. I have been waiting for you to come back to me for months! You have been going out, getting drunk, and not coming home for days, and now I find out you have been spending special nights with someone else! I want you to tell me something. If you can say no to this question, I won't go anywhere, and don't lie!" Then she asked, "Did you sleep with Billy?" I didn't say anything. I just put my head down. "Answer me, Carrie! I want to hear you say it. Tell me how you gave your body to someone else while I sat at home worrying if you were okay. Tell me how, while I was here crying myself to sleep, you were out fucking someone else!" She then became calm and said, "You know, I talked to my mom about what was going on and asked her what I should do. Do you know what she told me? She said to have a little patience. She said that you love me, and that you were hurting right now. She said that you would not hurt me intentionally, but I can see that she was wrong about this. You threw everything we had away. We have nothing left. Carrie, I did everything that I thought would make you happy, but I guess it wasn't good enough." Then she said, "So, Carrie, how many times did you sleep with him? Was he the only one? No, don't answer that. Once is enough for me. So that special night must have been the night you gave him your virginity!" As she was saying this tears were running down her face.

I ran to the bathroom, feeling myself getting sick. All I could think was *This is it; she's leaving me. It's over.* What was I going to do without my Kim? I couldn't even say she broke my heart; I had broken my own heart, along with Kim's. I didn't even know who I was anymore. I heard the front door close. When I went into the bedroom, Kim was gone. I went to the living room; no sign of her at all. I saw a note sitting on the kitchen counter that said, "I'll let you know when I'm coming to get the rest of my stuff. Please don't try to contact me. If you really love me, you'll leave me alone." All I could do was cry. I fell on the floor and cried until I passed out. When I woke up the next morning, I was still lying on the living room floor where I had cried myself to sleep.

Chapter Eleven

The Dance Is Over

I looked around the living room; it was so quiet, until I heard a knock at the door. I didn't want to see anyone, but I thought perhaps it was Kim, so I asked who it was.

A voice said, "It's Michelle."

I said, "Kim isn't here!"

Michelle said, "I know, Carrie. Open the door, please. I need to talk to you; it's important."

I opened the door and let her in. I told her to have a seat and that I would be right back. I went into the bathroom, washed my face, and brushed my teeth. When I came back into the living room, Michelle looked kind of strange. I sat down and said, "What do you need to talk to me about?"

"Kim wanted me to come and talk to you about some things."

"Okay, is she coming home?"

"I'm sorry, Carrie, she's not. She wanted you to know she would be paying the rent, up until the lease is up. So, that gives you five months here. She also paid your car note up to a year, so that gives you time to find a job and make payments. She wants you to know if you fall on hard times to let me know and I'll tell her. She will help you with anything you need. But you are not to contact her in any kind of way."

"Michelle, you have to know how sorry I'm and how much I love her. I would do anything to get her back. I messed up so badly. I love her and didn't mean to hurt her or betray her."

"I know, Carrie, but you really hurt her."

"I know, Michelle, and for that I'll always be sorry. Please tell her to come home. I'm going to die without her."

"Carrie, don't make me think you're going to hurt yourself."

"I already did when I lost Kim. My heart is dying. Michelle, I have no one. I don't even have anyone to talk to. I'm all alone."

Michelle said, "That's not true, Carrie. If you need someone to talk to, you can always call me. I'm your friend."

I sat there not saying anything. After Michelle left, I got into the bed and stayed there for the next four days. I didn't feel well and my heart was aching worse than it ever had before. I also felt as if I was getting the flu. My routine was the same for the next few weeks. I would wake up in the morning, go to the bathroom, throw up, lie back down in the bed, look at the empty spot where Kim used to lay, and cry myself right back to sleep.

A month had passed and I was still in bed, feeling hopeless. When I heard someone knocking at my door, I ignored it. While I was lying there one day, I heard someone come in the door. I was scared and could not move. I heard footsteps coming toward my room, so I pulled the cover up to my chin, and when the door opened, I saw that it was Michelle. I said, "You scared me, Michelle."

She said, "I came to check on you. You're not answering your phone or the door, so Kim gave me her keys. Carrie, how long have you been in this bed?"

"Since the day you left here."

Michelle was shocked and said, "Carrie, do you realize that was over a month ago? You need to get up and get yourself together."

"I'm sick; I think I have the flu."

"Yeah, you look bad. Sorry, Carrie, but maybe you should go to the doctor."

"No, I'm waiting to die!"

"Carrie, don't say that!"

"Michelle, what do I have to live for? I've lost everything that ever meant anything to me and that I love. Have you talked to Kim? How is she? I miss her so much, Michelle. I need her."

"Yes, you know I talk to Kim; she's not doing so well."

"She never came to get the rest of her stuff."

"Yeah, I know. She couldn't get herself to come over here."

"So, she doesn't want to see me, ever?"

"Look, Carrie, I can't answer that for her, but as of right now she can't see you. Remember you're not the only one hurting. Kim did nothing wrong. All she ever did was try to be there for you and love you."

"I know, Michelle. I'm ashamed of myself."

"Carrie, let's make you a doctor's appointment and I'll take you."

"I don't want to go!"

"Come on, Carrie, do this for me, okay?"

"All right fine, I'll make an appointment." I was feeling bad—my stomach was hurting and I was throwing up all the time. Michelle said, "You know I finally got Kim to go out to dinner, just to get her out of the house and we ran into Angie. She said, 'Kim, so you're single now? I saw your ex-girl making out with my friend Sandy about two months ago. She was so drunk, and I know she slept with Sandy, so that must mean you're single. When are you going to take me out?' Can you believe she asked Kim out, right in front of me?"

I panicked and said, "Oh my God! She's going out with Angie now?"

"No, don't be ridiculous. Kim would never do that. She was just hurt by what she heard you had done. I mean, how would you feel if this happened to you? Think about it, Carrie, all that love you were giving to Kim and she went out and betrayed you. Wouldn't you be hurt?"

"Of course I would! I'm hurting now, and I'm the one who caused it all!"

I got up to go to the bathroom and Michelle said, "Oh my God, have you been eating? You've lost so much weight!"

"I can't eat; I don't feel well."

She said, "Do you have any soup?"

"Yes, I think so. Why?"

"I'm going to make you some soup. You need to eat."

"I'm not hungry."

"You need to eat something. I'm going to make you some soup and watch you eat all of it."

I said, "Fine, I'll try."

She said, "Okay, Carrie, take a shower and I'll meet you in the living room."

So I jumped in the shower and when I came into the living room, Michelle had soup, orange juice, and some crackers ready for me. She made sure I ate all of it. Then she made me call to make a doctor's appointment. Next week, I was going to the doctor. In the meantime, I planned to spend all of my time sleeping. That way I didn't have to think about how I ruined my life or feel the pain in my heart.

I couldn't sleep that night, thinking about everything Michelle told me I had done and how badly I hurt Kim. So I got some paper and decided to write Kim a letter, hoping she would read it. But I could not figure out how to start my letter, so I let it come from my heart.

To Kim, the love of my life,

I want to start out by saying I'm very sorry

that I hurt you. I can't believe the things that

I did. You know in life, some people say you're not supposed to have regrets, but sitting here right now, I know that is not true in my case. If I could turn back the hands of time, I wouldn't have done any of those things I did to hurt you. I would change all of it. I now know what I had and what I lost. If someone walked up to me right now and said I could have my loving Kim back if I let them cut my arm off, I would cut it off myself and not think twice about it. I lay here looking at your side of the bed, embracing your pillow every day and night, wishing it was you. I know I hurt you deeply and for that I'm very sorry. I promise you, I did not do it with any sort of intent or on purpose, and I do understand why you left. Kim, as long as I don't have you in my life, I'll be paying for my mistakes. I had the most beautiful heart, when I had you. I cannot think of anything I can do to make it up to you, or any way to show you how sorry I am. If you know of a way, please let me know and I'll do anything you ask of me. I'll always love you, even if it has to be from afar. I miss you!

Your touch, your face, your smile, the way you would hold me and make love to me. I miss the way you would pull me into you when I would roll over as I was sleeping. I miss your smell, your lips, you waking me up in the morning with a kiss and saying, "Good morning, sleepyhead.

I love you." I miss the way you used to introduce me to everyone as your wife. I just miss all of you. You're all that makes sense to me. I have not tried to contact you because I want to honor your wishes. You said if I really love you, I would not contact you. So, again, I'm trying to prove my love to you, even if that means I have to cry myself to sleep every night, being without you. I keep taking myself back to a time when we were happy, just so I can have something to hold on to, but then I find myself right back in reality, which I call "My Hell." Where there's no Kim. I hear the words to that song I love so much when I think of you: "I would give anything I own, just to have you back again, just to touch you once again." I hate myself right now for what I did to you and if I could take your pain away, I would do it in a heartbeat. You know my mother has told me all of my life that I'm no good, and now I see why. Look what I did to you. I have proven her right! Now I know why she never wanted me around and why she cut me out of her life. I guess I can't blame her. When I was very young, my mom used to take a pillow and smother me to see if I would die, but I guess she didn't get lucky. I remember that so well. She would hold the pillow down as long as she could over my face, then when she would lift the pillow up to see me catching my breath, she would say, "You can't even die right." Then she would leave the room. I would cry, wondering what I could do to get her to love me. I guess I could never figure out how to do that. It seems like I searched most of my life for someone to love me, then when I finally did get the love that I needed, I threw it away over the one person who would not give it to me. Kim, I'm not trying to get your sympathy; it's just that Michelle told me that you blame yourself for what happened to us. I wanted you to see what you were dealing with, and that you did nothing wrong. Kim, I don't want you to hurt anymore. If there is anything I can do to take away any of the pain, please let me know. I'll do anything you ask of me. I'm going to end this letter. I think I said enough. If you get this letter, just know that I love you and always will.

Love,

The Carrie you

used to know

I'm really sorry,

baby. . . .

I took the letter and put it on the nightstand. Then I went to sleep. I had no idea what time it was when I woke up. I got up, went to the bathroom, and then checked the time. It was 10:00 p.m. I must have slept the whole day away again. I decided to make something to eat. I tried to eat my turkey burger, but I was still feeling sick. I went back to bed.

The whole week went by and then it hit me that I had a doctor's appointment the next day.

I knew I had to be ready when Michelle came to pick me up.

When I woke up the next morning, I got in the shower, got dressed, made some tea, and waited for Michelle. When she got here, she was surprised to see that I was ready to go. She came in, gave me a hug, and said, "How are you feeling?"

I said, "Still not well," and we headed out the door.

On the drive to my appointment, I wanted to ask about Kim, but I didn't want her to think this was why I was letting her take me to the doctor. When we arrived, I filled out all of the forms and handed them to the lady behind the counter along with my medical card. She told me to have a seat until I was called. Sounding somber, I said, "So Michelle, how have you been?"

She said, "I've been okay."

"How are you and Vanessa doing?"

"Everything is great. I'm going to ask her to move in with me."

"Wow, that's big. So, I guess you love her?"

"I more than love her; I'm in love with her. I was trying to take it slow. After all, look what happened with Angie."

I said, "Yeah, I can understand that. So when are you going to ask her?"

"Tomorrow night, I'm taking her to a special dinner because it's our anniversary."

"Congratulations. I wish you all the best and I hope it lasts a lifetime. You deserve it."

She said, "Thank you, Carrie."

I replied, "You're very welcome. I have a favor to ask of you."

She said, "Okay. What is it, Carrie?"

"Last week after you left, I wrote a letter to Kim. I was wondering if you could get it to her."

"Look, Carrie, she's doing a little better and I don't want to upset her. So I don't think that would be wise."

"I'll tell you what. Why don't you read it and if you think it's going to upset her then I won't send it to her, okay?"

She said, "Okay, Carrie."

I pulled the letter out of my purse. Michelle read it and agreed to give it to Kim but assured me she could not make her read it. I said, "Fair enough. Thanks, Michelle."

Then she looked at me with a sad look and said, "Carrie, your mother tried to kill you?"

"I don't really want to talk about it, please."

She put her arm around me and said, "Okay."

They called my name and I went in to see the doctor. They performed all kinds of tests, including that long overdue AIDS test. I sat there in that cold room with that gown on waiting for the doctor to come back. When he walked into the room, he had my chart in his hands. Looking down at it, he said, "You need to eat more. The reason you're not feeling well is that you're not eating enough for two."

I said, "Excuse me?"

He repeated himself, making it clearer this time. He said, "Carrie, you're about sixteen weeks pregnant. I'm going to prescribe you some prenatal vitamins, but you need to eat more. You really are eating for two now."

My heart was in my stomach and I couldn't think straight. The only thing going through my mind was *Oh my God! Oh my God! Oh my God!* Over and over again in my head.

He said, "I'll give your prescriptions to the nurse. You can pick them up after you get dressed."

I stood there not knowing what to do. I asked the nurse if I could see the doctor for a minute. When he returned, I asked him about having an abortion, but he said I was too far along, but if I was interested in adoption, he could refer me to someone. I was stunned. What was I going to do? How did I get here? How did I manage to turn my life upside down?

When I came out, Michelle was sitting reading a magazine. She saw me and jumped up. She said, "Is everything okay?"

I picked up my prescriptions and headed out the door. I said, "I really don't want to talk about it right now."

She said, "Okay, do you need me to take you to fill your prescriptions?"

"No, I'll do it later."

Then she asked, "Are you sure? I don't mind. I'm here to help you, Carrie."

I said, "No, but thanks. I'll get them later." I didn't say a word all the way home.

Michelle said, "Carrie, are you okay?" But I didn't hear her, so she grabbed my hand. She repeated, "Carrie, hello! Are you okay?"

"Um, yeah. I'll be fine. Thanks for taking me to the doctor. Take care."

I got out of the car so fast; I could tell she knew something was wrong. I jumped in my car and went straight to the drug store to get my prescriptions filled. While waiting for it, Michelle surprised me when she walked up to me.

"Did you follow me here?" I pleaded.

"Yes, I know something is wrong. Talk to me; I'm all you've got right now."

"I don't know what to say," and then they called my name.

When I walked up to the counter, the pharmacist said, loudly enough for everyone to hear, how many times a day I needed to take the prenatal pills.

I then heard Michelle say, "Oh my God! You're pregnant!"

I started crying and said, "Why do you think I was acting so strange when I came out of the doctor's office, and on the drive home? The doctor told me I'm too far along to get an abortion; I have no idea what I'm going to do besides lose my mind."

She said, "Okay, Carrie, I'll help you figure something out. Don't lose your mind; do your best to hang in there." She was saying all of this as she was hugging me.

"I can't ask you to do this; you have a lot going on. You're about to ask your girlfriend to move in with you. Plus, you're dealing with Kim. I think that's enough, so don't worry about me. I'll deal with it."

"Look, Carrie, I'm not going to leave you alone to deal with this by yourself."

I started freaking out. "Oh my God, you're not going to tell Kim, right? Promise me, please. I need to hear you say it! Please, Michelle, I'm begging you!"

Michelle said, "You know I just got her out of her slump and I'm not trying to put her back there. So, no, I'm not going to tell her, but I'm sure she will find out in time." Then she said, "Well, maybe she won't find out for a while. I'm not supposed to tell you this, but she's moving away. I can't tell you where and I won't be seeing her for a while, but she is going to stay in touch with me."

"When is she leaving, Michelle?"

"I can't tell you that, Carrie. Right now, you need to worry about what you're going to do. You're pregnant, and you really need to deal with that."

"Michelle, I really need Kim now."

"Look, Kim is dealing with her own stuff. Do you really want to hurt her more? She can't deal with you being pregnant."

"Michelle, I can't do this alone. I need Kim. Please tell her I need to talk to her."

"Calm down, Carrie. Take a deep breath. Everything is going to be okay. I'll help you; we'll take things one day at a time."

"I feel like my world has come to an end, like I have no idea what I'm going to do, or how I'm going to go on without Kim. I don't want this, I don't want any of this, and I'm going to lose it. Oh my God, why did I do this?"

Michelle hugged me until I stopped crying. "Come on, Carrie, you need to drive home. Let's go."

I drove home crying. When I got there, all I could think about was how I would never see Kim again, and how I had this life growing inside of me. I had no right to ask Kim to talk to me, but I needed her. I knew Kim would make everything okay. I could not believe she was leaving. No good-bye, no last hug, no last kiss, no last caress, and no last smile.

This was it; she was going to be gone out of my life for good. Tears filled my eyes once again as I thought of this. I knew I had to leave this place. I knew it wasn't good for me to stay in the place where I had lived with Kim and shared so much. But where would I go? Where would I live? How would I live and take care of a baby? After Michelle made sure I drove home from the drug store, she pulled up to me in the parking lot and said, "I'll be back in about an hour."

I was so hoping she would come back with Kim, but when she showed up with a bunch of groceries, all hope went out the window. I was very disappointed, but also grateful she was making sure I had enough to eat, not that I really wanted to eat. But now I had to, because I had to make sure the baby was okay.

"Michelle, do you think you can get Kim to see me one more time before she leaves? I won't say anything about her leaving. I just need to see her one more time. Michelle, please?"

"Here's what I'll do, Carrie. I'll give her your letter and ask her if she wants to see you before she leaves. If she says no, I'm not going to push her, okay?"

"Thank you!" I exclaimed.

"Hey, don't get too excited. I'm not sure if she will see you. If she does agree to it, your best bet is not to tell her you're pregnant, if you don't want to hurt her anymore."

"Okay, I won't say anything; I just want to see her."

"Carrie, I don't think you know how much you hurt her. There were nights I would have to stay up all night with Kim while she cried; she loved you more than life itself. I know you think about how your life has changed, but think about her. She thought nothing would come between the two of you, ever! I know on her part she made sure nothing did. I hate to tell you this, Carrie, but do you know how many times and how many girls used to come after her when she and I were out? But she never looked twice. She knew she had what she wanted. She was crazy about you! She fought to keep you even when you didn't trust her. She did things that other people would have given up on.

"Right before Christmas, when you two went up to L.A., before you found out your mother was gone, Kim had planned to buy you two a house. But while getting all of that ready, you started acting up. Going out all the time and doing whatever it was that you were doing. She was going to have a marriage ceremony for you two and then take you on a honeymoon. Don't you see Carrie? You were her life. You were everything to her, and she lost everything she ever wanted in life. Now look at everything. She's just trying to get through this, and that's why she's moving away."

"Why can't we try again?"

"I can't answer that for Kim, but I can tell you this. Once you hurt someone, things change between the two of you. There's no more trust and it's important to have trust. Without trust, you can't have a real relationship. Think about how hard it would be for Kim to trust you. She would always be thinking about you sleeping with other people. How would you feel if I told you Kim was sleeping with someone else right now?"

"Is she sleeping with someone else? Michelle, tell me! Tell me she's not, please!"

Michelle said, "You see how that makes you feel?"

I said, "Yes, it hurts."

"So, imagine how she's feeling. If you two got back together, she would always be worried where you're going every time you walked out the door. I don't think either of you could live like that."

"But I love her."

"And you had that love for a long time, and then you threw it away. If you really love her, you'll let her go."

"I know what you're saying is probably best, but it doesn't change the way I feel."

"I know, but you're going to have to accept it for now. Here's what you need to do, Carrie. You're having a baby. You need to focus on that. Are you going to tell the father?"

I didn't answer her.

She said, "Okay, I'm not trying to be mean, but do you know who the father is?"

I said, "No, I don't."

"Okay, Carrie, do you plan to find out who the father is?"

"No, I would have to go on a talk show for the results of that answer. I need some time to think about what I'm going to do."

Then Michelle said, "Oh shit, it's after eight! I have to run, I'm late. Vanessa is going to kill me! I was supposed to pick her up at seven thirty and I haven't even taken a shower yet."

"Why don't you call her and I'll let her know it's my fault."

"No, that's okay, she's very understanding. I'll call her on my way home. I have to go. I'll talk to you tomorrow. In the meantime, call me if you need me."

"Okay, Michelle, thanks for everything."

She hugged me then left. Once again I found myself alone. I looked around the room and started missing Kim. Yearning for those days when it was just she and I, spending time alone. Everything in the house reminded me of her. I took my pills and went to bed. Of course it took me forever to fall asleep. I grabbed Kim's pillow and hugged it until I fell asleep. One thing I knew for sure, I would never love anyone the way I loved Kim.

Three days later, I decided to keep my baby as opposed to giving it up for adoption. When I called Michelle to tell her, she said, "Whatever you want to do, I'll support you." Then I asked her if she gave Kim the letter. She said, "Yes, I did, and she read it, but she didn't say anything to me about it. She just said that she had read it."

"Did you ask her if I could see her one more time before she left?"

Michelle said, "I'm sorry, Carrie, she's gone."

I just lost it. I threw the phone. I knew Michelle could hear me screaming in the background. I started tearing up the house and yelling, "I hate myself!" and "Why, God?"

Ten minutes later I heard Michelle banging at the door, but I wasn't letting her in. That was it. I was done. I didn't want to live anymore; my heart hurt too much.

"Go away; it's all over!" I yelled. I went into the bathroom to find a razor blade. That was it. I was going to a place where I would feel no more pain, but I couldn't do it knowing I had a baby inside of me. So I sat there in the bathroom on the floor in a daze. Then I heard Michelle coming through the door. I forgot she had keys, but she must have broken the chain off the door to get in.

She came into the bathroom and saw me sitting there with a razor blade in my hand. She got me off the floor, took the blade from me, and sat me down in the bedroom on the bed. She said, "We need to get you some help. It's not just you anymore; there's a baby that didn't ask for this and you need to get it together. So if that means going to get help, then that's just what you'll do!"

"I don't want any help. I want to die without hurting the baby."

"You know that's not possible, Carrie. You're not making any sense. Come on, let's go."

"Where are we going?" I asked.

"To the hospital. You need help."

"No, I don't! I need Kim!" I shouted.

"She's gone, Carrie, we need to get you there. Come on, get dressed."

"No! I don't want to!" I yelled.

"Stop yelling, Carrie; do this for the baby. Come on, it's going to be okay."

"It will never be okay. I lost Kim. Everything is over. Don't you understand that?" I started getting frantic. "Where did Kim go? Tell me, Michelle. I'll go to her. Please, Michelle." I was crying hysterically. "I need Kim, please. Michelle, I'll do anything. I need her. Help me, Michelle. Tell me where she is."

"Carrie, this isn't good for the baby. Come on, get yourself together, please!"

"I'm losing my mind! Can't you see that? Michelle, please, can't you call her and let me hear her voice? I want to hear her voice."

Michelle said, "Carrie, you know I can't do that. You need to let her go, she's not coming back."

I was getting angry. I said, "Don't tell me that; she loves me. She's the only one, Michelle." I didn't even know if Michelle understood half of what I was saying.

Michelle started crying and said, "I knew I shouldn't have told you she was leaving. This is my fault."

Still crying, I said, "Oh my God, help me. I can't go on. This isn't right. I love Kim. I need Kim. Help me, God. Please, bring her back to me. I'll do anything you want, God, please." With tears flowing down my face, I lied on the floor. I couldn't move. Everything inside of me was gone. Anything that made sense was gone out of my head and my heart. I was so hurt. I couldn't feel anymore. This was it; I was going to die right there on the floor, right in front of Michelle.

I guess I must have passed out. The next thing I heard were voices, a man and a woman. I opened my eyes and looked around. I was in the hospital. I looked to see who the doctor was talking to. I assumed it was Michelle, but it was April, Kim's mom. What was she doing here after I hurt her daughter? I couldn't believe she was here. Maybe she was here to tell me off, and to tell me to leave her daughter alone.

When April noticed my eyes open, she said, "Hi, sweetheart, how are you feeling?" All I said was, "I'm so sorry, I didn't mean to hurt Kim; you have to believe me. I love her."

She interrupted me and started hugging me. As I cried, she said, "It's okay, Carrie, everything is going to be fine. You just need to get some rest."

I was wondering if she knew that I was pregnant. If she didn't know, once she found out, would she hate me? Why was she here and who told her where I was?

Michelle came in the room and said, "Hey, Carrie, how are you feeling?" I looked down and said nothing.

April's phone rang. "I'll be right back," she said.

When she left the room I asked Michelle, "What is Kim's mom doing here?"

"I had to call her, Carrie. You need all the support you can get. When I told her what was happening, she got on a plane from New York right away and came to see you."

"Does she know what happened?"

"Yes, she knows everything; you know Kim tells her mom everything."

"But Kim doesn't know that I'm pregnant."

"No, but I told April, so she knows about the baby. She wants you to get better. She knows you don't really have anybody and she said you'll always be her family. So as family, she is here for you. I don't think you know how much she loves you. We're going to help you get better and then you're going back with her to New York. While she does her play, you'll be staying with her in her condo."

"What about Kim? Won't she get mad?"

"No, she knows, but she won't be coming around. I hate to tell you that, but I don't want you to get your hopes up. Now let's concentrate on getting you better."

"I'm not sure if I'll get better, Michelle."

"Yes, you will. Remember—one day at a time, okay?"

"Okay, I'll try." Then Michelle said, "If you don't, I'll kill you myself!" Michelle was trying to lighten the mood.

Two weeks went by and they had me talking to a psychiatrist every day. April and Michelle visited me every day at the hospital. April talked about our plans she had for us in New York. She assured me everything would be okay and that she would help me with everything. Michelle told me how much she would miss me and made me promise to call her every week.

Michelle came to me a few days before I was leaving and said, "Carrie, Vanessa knows that you don't know her very well, but she would like to come by and see you before you go. Is that okay?"

I said, "Sure, it's okay."

On my last day, Vanessa came by to see me. She asked if she could speak to me alone for a few minutes. Everyone left the room to give us some privacy.

"Carrie, I know you don't know me that well, but I wanted to take a few minutes of your time. I kind of know what you're going through. You see, I had this girlfriend that I loved very much, but I made a mistake. I also cheated like you did. I was out with some friends, we were drinking, and I got so drunk that I had no idea what I was doing. My girlfriend at the time would do anything for me. We were inseparable. I thought no one could tear us apart. But this one girl in particular, who really wanted my girlfriend, set me up. She got some of her friends to befriend me. Her plan was to have me cheat with one of them. That way, she could have a clear path to my girlfriend. Unfortunately, what I didn't know was, they spiked my drink. The next thing I knew, I woke up in bed with one of her friends. To make a long story short, the girl told my girlfriend and I lost her forever. I thought I would never get through that heartbreak, but in time, I did. I know right now it seems like it's going to hurt forever, but time will take that pain away."

I said, "You got drunk, Vanessa? I can't see you doing that."

"You know, Carrie, everybody makes mistakes. We're all human."

I thought about what she said and thanked her.

"I'm going to give you my number, so if you ever want to talk, you can call me, any time. I'm also going to pray for you and your baby." She gave me a hug and said, "We're all here for you!"

When Michelle came in, I told her to come closer. I whispered in her ear, "You have a good one; don't let her get away."

She smiled and said, "I won't." As I got everything packed in the hospital, I told April I needed to get some stuff from my place. She told me everything had been shipped to New York and was already waiting for me, and anything else I needed, we would buy. She also told me all of the furniture was put in storage and she would be paying that bill every month. Michelle would be taking my car up to Los Angeles and it would be at April's house. So here I was, moving to New York with the love of my life's mother. I was starting a completely new life.

We got our seats on the plane; first class, of course. April wouldn't have it any other way. She got me some water and crackers, just in case I got morning sickness, and told me to take a nap. I tried to sleep, but I couldn't. I looked out the window.

Turning to April, I asked, "Why are you doing this for me?"

"My daughter loves you and I love you. I told you I'm your family. I know you hurt Kim, but I also know it wasn't intentional. Right now Kim is hurting, but through all her hurt, she still cares what happens to you and so do I, sweetheart. I don't think you have any idea how much Kim loves you. In time, maybe you two can sit down and talk, maybe even become friends. Who knows what the future holds."

"Can I ask you something, April?"

"Sure, you can ask me anything."

"Does Kim know that I'm pregnant?"

"No, she doesn't, and I'm not going to tell her unless she asks. I don't want to lie to her."

I asked, "How is she holding up?"

"She's doing a lot better, so I'm sure in time she will be fine. But I want you to concentrate on you and the baby for now.

Chapter Twelve

I Never Knew It Could Be Like This

While I'm Missing You

When we got to the condominium in New York, I saw that it was big and beautiful and right in the heart of Manhattan. It was around five thousand square feet and had three bedrooms, four bathrooms, and an office. April showed me to my room. The room was fit for a princess, but it still felt strange being with Kim's mom. After I got all settled in, Kim's mom took me out to dinner to a nice place called Balthazar, where the cute waiters served the oysters Kim's mom loved so much. She made sure I got something healthy. When we got back to the condo, she asked me if I needed anything.

I said, "No, thank you."

"Tomorrow we're going shopping, so be ready at ten a.m. I love shopping for baby stuff, and I know we're going to have so much fun." I smiled at her when she said that.

The next day, we had a big breakfast. I was so full, she let me rest for a while, and then we went out shopping. There were some really cute baby shops on Fifth Avenue and we had a ball. Around 2:00 p.m., April asked if I was ready for some lunch, but I told her I was still full from the big breakfast.

She said, "Okay, let's at least go and get some smoothies."

I said, "Okay, sounds great." We shopped around a little more; I was exhausted when I got home.

A week and a half passed and I was having so much fun, although I found myself caught in a moment, thinking about how this could have been Kim and me both, raising a family together. I could see her rubbing and kissing my stomach, saying, "This is my baby." I know we would have had a good life together, if I hadn't fucked everything up! I was wondering where she was and if she was happy now. Did she have a girlfriend, or was she dating? Was she taking some time for herself and was she missing me? I wondered if she even thought about me.

While we were out one day, April got a call and told me she had to take it. She said she would be right back and stepped outside of the store to talk. I wondered if it was Kim. Who was I kidding? Every time April's phone rang, I wondered if it was Kim. I wondered if I would ever talk to or see Kim again, although spending time with her mother made me feel closer to her.

One night while I was lying in bed, I started missing Kim so much, I started crying. April must have heard me, because she came in my room and sat down on my bed.

She said, "Everything is going to be okay."

I said, "I miss Kim so much."

She said, "I know, sweetheart, but she can't see you right now."

"You know I can't ever be happy without Kim."

She said, "We need you to concentrate on the baby for now."

I said, "She doesn't love me anymore, does she?"

"Sweetheart, it's because she does love you, that she can't see you right now. Did you call Michelle this week?"

I said, "No."

She said, "Then why don't you call her to get your mind off of the sad things, and see what's going on with her and her girlfriend."

With that said, I wiped my eyes and called Michelle.

"Hello?" I heard a voice say.

I said, "Michelle?"

The voice on the other end said, "No, hold on a second," and then Michelle came on and said, "Hello."

"Hello, Michelle how are you?"

Michelle sounded surprised to hear from me. She said, "Oh, Carrie, I'm doing fine. How are you and the baby doing?"

"We're doing okay. So what have you been up to, and how's Vanessa?"

"We're doing well. That was her who answered the phone. What have you been up to?"

"I've been having lots of fun. When April isn't working, she takes me out shopping for the baby, or out to dinner. It's nice being here. You should see her condo. It's so beautiful! My room is huge. She lets me do whatever I want as long as it doesn't hurt me or the baby. Tomorrow she's taking me to her rehearsal. I've never been to a rehearsal before, let alone Broadway. I'm also going to her opening night; I'm so excited!"

Michelle said, "Well, that sounds great. I'm glad you're doing so well and I miss you."

I said, "I miss you, too. Can I speak to Vanessa?"

She said, "Sure, hold on."

When she got on the phone, she said, "Hey, Carrie, how are you?"

"I'm good, Vanessa, but I have my moments."

Vanessa said, "Yeah, I remember those days. I still get them every once in a while. Don't get me wrong, I love Michelle and would never do anything to mess up what I have with her. You know we live together now."

"That's great. I'm so happy for you, but can I ask you a question?"

She said, "Sure, anything."

"Do the moments ever stop?"

"So far, no, but they do get easier to deal with. Just try to think about the good times and it will get easier, you'll see."

"Okay, thanks."

"Michelle is asking to speak to you again. It's been great talking to you. Now, don't forget to call me if you want to talk, okay?"

"Okay, I will."

When Michelle got back on the phone she said, "Hey, Carrie, hold on. I need to tell you something and I don't want Vanessa to hear me."

"Okay."

Then she came back on and said, "Everything is going so good with Vanessa, so I'm going to ask her to marry me."

"Wow, that's great! Michelle, I'm so happy for you."

"Yeah, I bought a ring. I'm just hoping she likes it. Better yet, I'm hoping she says yes!"

"I'm sure she will love the ring and she will marry you in a heartbeat. She loves you. Call me and let me know how it goes, okay?"

"I sure will."

"Hey, Michelle, I also want to thank you for all of your help. You're a good friend and I really love you!"

"Hey, that's what friends are for. You can call me anytime you need me."

"Well, it's late here and I need to get my rest. It was great talking to you. I'll call you soon."

"Okay, love you, bye."

I laid back in bed and went to sleep.

The next day April said we needed to leave early so we could get a new dress for opening night of her play. We went to a private shop where they apparently were waiting for us; they had five dresses waiting for me to try on. They were all so beautiful. After I picked the pretty Donna K. dress, we went and picked out shoes, then headed to Broadway. I was in awe, watching April rehearse her part. After watching April in rehearsal, I could not stop talking about opening night. She loved that I was so excited! The next morning when I got up, April was gone. There was a note that said,

"I have a breakfast date, and then I'm going to rehearsal.
I'll see you tonight, and make sure you eat!"

Love you ☺

I ate breakfast, and then I went for a walk to check out the neighborhood. It was so busy on the streets. I headed back home and watched TV for the rest of the day. When April got back, I was sleeping. So I never saw her that day, but while sleeping I felt her come in my room and kiss me on the cheek.

Weeks were going by. I had not heard anything about Kim and I was missing her like crazy. When April wasn't home, I looked at Kim's pictures that were around the place. I would kiss them and say, "I love you. I miss you so much. I'm so sorry, baby." I sat and talked to my baby inside of me. I told my baby I would not treat him or her the way my mom had treated me. I told my baby I was going to love him or her like crazy and make sure they were happy.

One night, April came home to find me talking to my baby. I looked up and saw her smiling at me.

She said, "That's right, talk to your baby and tell your baby we're going to make sure he or she has a very good life." She then sat down next to me and started rubbing my stomach and said, "This baby needs you and will love you no matter what. So get ready to be wanted and needed like crazy. It's the best feeling in the world to have. Most people take it for granted, but I'm going to help you see your blessings."

I went to bed that night with something to look forward to, my blessings. When I woke up in the morning, April had made breakfast and told me a car was coming to pick me up, taking me to get my hair done for the big night. I asked if she was going with me and she said, "Sorry, I can't. I have a lunch date, so I'll see you tonight at the show."

I noticed she was having a lot of dates lately, but I didn't want to seem nosey, so I didn't ask about the mystery man. We ate breakfast together, and then she told me to get ready. She hugged me and said, "Call me if you need me," then she was out the door.

I got in the shower and got dressed, and about twenty minutes later, a buzz sounded at the door. It was the doorman telling me my car was here. I grabbed my purse and headed out the door. While I was getting my hair done, I was so excited thinking about the opening that night. I loved my dress so much and I couldn't wait to wear it. So when I got home, I pulled it out of the closet just to look at it. I was hoping it still fit since my stomach was getting bigger. I was really beginning to look pregnant now. I had that rounded stomach that you see when a woman is going to have her baby. My stomach all of a sudden popped out. I ate some lunch, and then took a nap. When my alarm went off, it was time for me to get ready. I was so excited! I got into the shower, and just as I was getting out, the phone rang. I went to get it, but the person hung up. I had finished getting ready when a buzz sounded at the door again. The doorman told me my car was here. Just as I was getting into the car, my cell phone rang again. I said, "Hello?"

"Hey, sweetheart, it's April. Are you on your way?"

"Yes, I just got in the car. I'm glad you called, because I wanted to tell you to break a leg."

Then she laughed. She said, "Oh, that's sweet, but with my luck, I just might. Okay, sweetheart, your ticket is at will-call. Give them your name, and they will have your ticket. After the show ends, come backstage. If anyone tries to stop you, tell them who you are and they will let you into my dressing room."

When I pulled up in the car, it was so exciting. The lights were all lit up, and they were lighting up what seemed like the whole block. I got out of my car and went to will-call. When I got inside and showed my ticket, an usher showed me to my seat in the balcony. It was a full house. The show was sold out. I couldn't believe I wasn't only there, but in a private balcony. The lights went down, and then they began to flicker. The show was starting. Everyone clapped and the curtains opened. It was so great. When intermission came, I didn't want to leave my seat. When the lights began to flicker again, I was ready for the second half. It was a great night; the only thing that would have made it better was if Kim had been there with me.

When the play was over, the cast received a standing ovation. It was great! But then I spotted someone walking up to the stage, handing April some flowers. I started clapping more, but when I looked again at the person who gave April the flowers, I was stunned. My heart dropped when I realized it was Kim! I had to see her! I tried working my way down to the front of the stage, but it was so crowded, it took me forever to get there. When I finally got to the front, she was nowhere to be found. I thought maybe she went to her mom's dressing room, so I went backstage and told the guard who I was and he let me in. When I got to April's dressing room, she got up and hugged me. I looked around the room, but only saw a bunch of people from the play.

April said to me, "You look so pretty. Did you enjoy the show?"

I kept looking around the room, in case I didn't see Kim the first time. I said, "Yes, it was great! I loved it, thank you." I took April's hand, pulled her to the side, and said, "Where is she?" April said, "Where is who?"

"I saw her, I know I did. I saw her hand you flowers. Where is Kim?"

April said, "I'm sorry, sweetheart. She left. She didn't want to stick around and upset you."

The more I thought about it, the more obvious it became who April's dates were with. But where was she staying? And was she living here in New York, or did she show up just for her mother's play? I had to keep my cool. I was backstage at April's play, but I had to see her. Then I looked down at my big stomach. Would she be in shock if she saw that I was pregnant? I was so antsy April noticed and held my hand while she talked to people coming in to see her. She introduced me as her daughter to everyone she talked to. I wanted to run outside and find Kim, but I knew that wasn't going to happen.

When it was time to go to the opening-night party, I didn't have it in me. I asked April if she would be highly disappointed if I went back to the condo to rest.

She said, "No, I understand. I'll see you in the morning."

I said, "I'm really sorry; I just can't do this right now."

She said, "Sweetheart, it's okay. You go get some rest and everything will be okay." When I got back to the condo, I undressed and sat on the edge of the bed. I noticed an envelope with my name on it. I opened it and began to read the letter inside.

Dear Carrie,

When I saw you get out of that car in front of the box office, all the love I had for you came back. I saw that face and I remembered you. I remembered all those days and nights we spent together; that was the happiest time in my life. I wanted to run up to you and embrace you. I really wish it hadn't ended, but I guess everything comes to an end at some point. I have to say, you make a beautiful pregnant woman. You look lovely tonight. Yes, I know you're pregnant. My mother had to tell me in case I ran into you at the play, so I wouldn't be in shock. I think you will be a beautiful mother. Just take all of that love you have inside of you and give it to your baby. That was one of the things I loved about you. You always had a big heart; never forget that.

I know you must think that I hate you, but that could not be further from the truth. I still love you and that will never change. It's just that our relationship changed and I can't deal with that right now. Maybe someday I'll get over it and be able to see you and talk to you. I've talked to Michelle and she says you sound great. I'm happy for you, if that's true. I just wish I could have been the one who kept you happy.

I know this has to be hard on you and you must be scared, but don't worry, my mom will help you 100%. She loves having you there with her. She tells me she can't wait until her grandchild is born. You know, when she first told me that you were having a baby, I must say I was upset. But, then I thought about it. It's your life and you have moved on, as I'm trying to do, but that doesn't make it hurt any less.

Do you remember when we used to talk about having kids, and how we were going to raise them to love everyone? We were going to have two, one named Kim Jr. and the other named Carrie

Jr. Wow, we were crazy together. I miss those days. I miss you.

With that said, I want to thank you for all the happy years

you gave me; I'm just sorry it had to end this way. I'll never forget

you and as I said before, I'll always love you. Thank you for the

dance." I have to go. My mom just called and told me you're on your

way home and says you're not feeling well. I hope you feel better

soon. Take care.

Love Always,

The Kim you

used to know

I took the letter and clutched it to my heart. All I could think was that Kim was here and I missed her. It was so bittersweet; I had finally heard from her, but I didn't get to see her.

When I woke up in the morning, the letter was still in my hands. I was holding it to my heart. I could hear April on the phone due to my bedroom door being slightly open. I got up, washed my face, brushed my teeth, and went into the dining room where breakfast was waiting for me.

When she hung up the phone, I asked her if I could have a moment of her time, so she sat down next to me. "April, I wanted to thank you for everything. I know I'm not your responsibility to take care of, but you took me in even after I hurt your own daughter. I don't know anyone who would do that." Then I started getting choked up while I was talking to her, so she grabbed my hand as she listened to me talk. "I want you to know, I thank God every morning for sending you to me. Sometimes I find myself crying, because it's hard to believe I'm here with you. I know he sent his best angel to me, and for that I'll forever be grateful. You have shown me things and taken me places I thought I wouldn't see in a million years. You've bought me so much stuff and I don't deserve it. In only a few months, you have done what my mom has not done my entire life; and that's given me love. So, thank you. Thank you for everything, I mean it from the bottom of my heart. I love you."

She hugged me and said, "You are my daughter now and have been for a long time now. I love you and will always be here for you, Carrie. Besides, I have to. You're carrying my first grandchild and for that, I'll always be grateful. So thank you."

Then we laughed.

"Have you come up with any names for your first grandchild?"

"Well, when we find out what you're having, I'll come up with a name for my grandbaby."

I said, "Okay, I'm going to hold you to that. I have a doctor's appointment in three days, and I'm going to find out then, so you'd better be ready."

She said, "Why didn't you tell me? What time is your appointment? I'm going with you."

I said, "You don't have to, you've done enough."

She said, "Are you kidding? I wouldn't miss that! I'm going to find out what sex my grandbaby will be." Then she changed the subject. "So, Kim left you a letter?"

"Yeah."

"Are you okay with it?"

"Kind of."

"What's wrong?"

"I just wish I could have talked to her."

April said, "Give her some time." April was reassuring and said, "I know Kim, and she'll come around. It may be a long time from now, or it could be tomorrow, but she will come around. I know my baby; she just wishes it were her baby inside of you. I mean, she knows she

206

can't get you pregnant, but she always wanted a family with you, but not this way."

"I know. we used to talk about it all the time." I pulled the letter out of my pocket and said, "I want you to read it."

She said, "No, that's private."

I said, "It's okay, I want you to."

So she read it and said, "Yeah, you can hear the love she still has for you in her letter. That's why she can't see you. It's still too hard for her."

"I feel bad that she can't come and see you at home because I'm here," I said.

April replied, "Are you kidding? I put Kim up in her favorite plush hotel while she's here and she loves it." Then she said, "You know when I had those lunch, dinner, and breakfast dates? They were with Kim."

I said, "Yeah, I figured it out after I read her letter. I just wish I could have been there. I don't think I'll ever stop missing her, and I know I'll never stop loving her."

"I know, sweetheart. And I know she will never stop loving you. You know we're going back to Los Angeles in a month, when my play is over, right?"

I said, "Okay, but where am I going?"

"You're going home with me, silly. I was thinking you could live with me until the baby is born and then if you want to get your own place after that, I'll understand. But you should know if you move out, I'll be at your house all the time, visiting my grandbaby."

I said, "You can't take care of us forever."

She looked at me very seriously and said, "Who is going to stop me?"

I just laughed. She was so funny sometimes. I loved April. She always had a way of making me forget my problems for the moment. Being with April made me see why I loved her daughter so much. I figured when Kim left San Diego, she came here, to her mother. I know that's what I would have done, because April always made everything okay.

I said, "April, why is it that most of the time, we can't see what we have until it's gone?"

She said, "Well, how can you know what's good if you don't go through the bad?"

"I don't know. I guess you're right."

Then April said, "Unfortunately, sometimes we don't get a second chance. Come over to the living room, I want you to listen to something. Maybe it will help you to understand a little more." Then she put a CD in the player. The song was called "The Dance" by Garth Brooks. When I heard it, I cried and understood what she meant. The song was about the most loving relationship, which is called "The Dance." I had never heard a relationship referred to as a dance, but I liked it. What I got from it was, if you knew all your loving times were going to end badly before you took that "dance," would you still take it? In anything you do, there is no good without the bad. Once you get that, then you understand. I thought about it. Would I take that dance or that journey as April also referred to it? I found that question hard to answer. And now I knew why Kim said at the end of her letter, "Thank you for the dance." So, would I have taken that dance with Kim, knowing it would end up this way? How does one answer that question? It's not that easy. I wondered if Kim still would have taken the dance. All I knew was that I loved her and I would never stop loving her.

April was just full of information. I loved talking to her. After we talked, we headed out for smoothies. While we were out, April got a call. I heard her say, "What's wrong, baby?" Then she put one of her fingers up as a gesture to say, "Hold on," as she walked away from me. When she came back, she said, "I have to go. I'm going to put you in a cab." I asked if everything was okay. She said, "I'm not sure." Then she put me in a cab and I was headed home. I wondered what had happened. Was it Kim and was she okay? I was worrying the rest of the day.

It started to get late and I knew I wouldn't see April for the rest of the night, because she was doing her play. I sat there feeling nervous, and then I turned on the TV to take my mind off what happened. Then all of a sudden a newsbreak came on, saying the famous actress April Springs' daughter was rushed to the hospital. News at 11:00!

That was all they said when I freaked out and immediately tried calling April. She wasn't answering her phone. I was so scared wondering if Kim was okay. I didn't know what to do. I called Michelle, but she didn't answer either. I left her a message telling her what happened. I had to stay calm because of the baby, but I was so worried that something bad had happened to Kim. I heard it for myself on the news. I just wished they had said what happened to her! It was driving me crazy. I was walking around in circles and I started praying, "Please, God, let her be okay." Then my phone rang; it was Michelle.

"Hey, Carrie, I got your message, but I don't understand it. What did you say happened to Kim?"

"That's just it, I don't know what happened. I was out with April when all of a sudden she got this phone call. All I heard April say was 'Baby, I can't understand you when you're crying. Calm down and tell me what happened.' Then April said, 'Okay, I'm on my way.' Next thing I knew she put me in a cab and sent me home. When I got home, I was worried, which I knew wasn't good for the baby. So to take my mind off it, I turned the TV on and a newsbreak that said the famous actress April Springs' daughter was rushed to the hospital. News at eleven. I tried calling April, but she didn't answer her phone. Can you call her and see if Kim is okay? I'm freaking out. Look, you don't even have to tell me what happened to her. I need to know she's okay. Please, Michelle."

"Calm down, Carrie. I'll try to find out what's going on, and I'll call you back."

I said, "Okay, and don't forget!"

She said, "I won't. I'll call you as soon as I know something."

I waited and waited. It was close to midnight and Michelle still hadn't called. Finally, just after 1 a.m., my phone rang. It was April.

She said, "Hey, sweetheart, did I wake you?"

"No, I've been waiting to hear if Kim's okay. I watched the news when they said Kim was rushed to the hospital. Is she okay? Please tell me she's okay."

April said, "Those stupid reporters! What did they say?"

I spoke really fast trying to hurry so she could tell me if Kim was okay. I said, "There was a newsbreak that said the famous actress April Springs' daughter was rushed to the hospital. News at eleven, but when the eleven o'clock news came on, they said you had to be replaced with your understudy, due to your daughter being rushed to the hospital and that was it. Is she okay?"

April said, "Yes, she's fine. She's just going through a rough time. I'm going to stay here with her overnight and I'll see you tomorrow. Call me if you need anything."

I said, "Okay, I will." Knowing I wouldn't be able to sleep, I stayed up all night. I tried to sleep at one point, but I couldn't. I was still awake at 5 a.m. Then finally I must have nodded off because I heard voices all of a sudden. I looked at the time, and it was 11:30 a.m. April came in to my room to check on me.

She said, "Are you okay? It's almost lunchtime and you're still in bed. Have you gotten up and eaten anything yet?"

"No, I just woke up. I couldn't sleep last night. I was worried, so I finally fell asleep this morning around five a.m."

April said, "Okay, well, you know that's not good for the baby, so I'm going to get you some breakfast, then you can go back to sleep."

I asked, "How is Kim doing? Is she okay?"

April said, "Yes, she's going to be fine. Everything is going to be fine, for all of us."

Chapter Thirteen

Under the Same Roof

"You just rest," April said. "You know you have a doctor's appointment tomorrow and I don't want you in there feeling tired. I want to hear from the doctor that you and the baby are doing just fine."

I said, "Okay, I will." While lying in bed, I heard April talking to someone in the next room. I really couldn't make out what they were saying, or if it was a man or a woman. The walls in the condo were so thick that all I heard were muffled voices. About twenty minutes later, April came in with some breakfast for me and told me I had to eat it all, so I did. After that she made me take a nap. I must have slept all day because I was starving when I woke up. When I looked at the time, it said 8:07 p.m. I couldn't believe I had slept all day; I hadn't done that since I left Los Angeles. I got up, went into the bathroom, and took a shower. On one of our shopping sprees, April bought me a bunch of maternity clothes. So I put on one of my short sets. It was a warm night; a good night for shorts. My plan was to get something to eat.

I heard April talking to someone in the living room. When I came out of the room, I was so shocked when I saw who it was, I literally fainted. When I came to, I was back in my bed and April was leaning over me, wiping my forehead with a cold rag and calling my name. She said, "Are you okay?"

"Yes, I thought I saw someone. I'm sorry."

She said, "It's okay. You did see who you thought you saw. Kim is here. I needed her to come home. She's been here all day while you were sleeping. I was going to tell you when you woke up."

"Did she leave or is she here?" I was so confused.

April said, "Yes, she is still here, but you need to concentrate on you and the baby. Now, how do you feel?"

"I feel okay, just a little confused."

She said, "What do you mean confused?"

"I don't know, I guess I was wondering if she's okay with me being here, while she's here."

April said, "Yes, sweetheart, she's okay. I needed to bring her home. Maybe I should take you to the hospital to get checked out."

"No, I'm fine. Besides, I have that doctor's appointment tomorrow, so I can get checked out then.

"Okay, but if you start to feel dizzy or if you get any pain, you let me know, okay? Promise me?"

"Okay, I promise."

Then I heard a light knock at the door and Kim saying in a whisper, "Hello. Is it okay to come in?"

April said, "Come on in, babe. And then I saw her face. She still looked beautiful to me. I know it hadn't been that long, but to me, it seemed like a lifetime since I'd seen her. She had a black eye. I was wondering what happened to her. She had on some jeans, a cute red top and she was carrying a cup of tea.

She said, "I made you some tea. I didn't mean to upset you. I know you're pregnant and I'm very sorry."

I couldn't say anything. I just stared at her.

Then April said, "Are you okay?"

I stuttered and said, "Yeah, I mean, yes."

Kim said, "How do you feel?"

I said to her, "Okay." I could barely even speak.

Then April said, "I made dinner. I made your favorite— spaghetti!"

I smiled and said, "Thank you," but then looked at Kim.

She was smiling and said, "Yeah, I remember you always had me make that for you." I still couldn't really say anything. Then Kim said, "Don't worry, Mom, I'll go and get it."

She left the room and April said, "Wow, you're really at a loss for words."

"I know, she does that to me. April, why does Kim have a black eye? Who hurt her pretty face? What happened to her?"

She said, "I can't tell you that, but if you want, you can ask Kim. It's up to her if she wants to tell you."

Kim came back in the room with a tray full of spaghetti. I loved it so much, because her mom made it spicy.

April's phone rang and she left the room. I was nervous. I didn't know what to do. Kim sat on the edge of the bed saying, "Come on and eat. I know the baby is hungry."

I looked at her and said, "Okay," then asked her, "How are you feeling, Kim?"

She said, "I'm okay, just tired."

I said, "Well, don't let me hold you up; why don't you go get some rest?" I said that to her, but I really wanted her to stay there with me all night. It felt so great having her there, I wished she would crawl in the bed with me and hold me all night like the good old days.

She said, "I'm going to bed soon; I wanted to make sure you were okay first."

I said, "Well, now you know I'm fine, why don't you go get some rest?"

She got up and said, "Okay. Good night." Then she peeked back in and said, "My mom is leaving soon to go to her play. So if you need anything, I'll be in the next room."

I said, "Okay, and thanks," and she left the room.

Wow, even though we were not in the same room or the same bed, I couldn't believe Kim and I were under the same roof. Kim was actually sleeping a few feet away from me.

April came back into the room and said, "Sweetheart, I'm running late. But if you need me call me, okay? Are you going to be okay with Kim in the next room?"

"Yes, she is going to sleep, and don't worry, I won't bug her."

She said, "I know you won't. Just remember to get some rest. We have that doctor's appointment tomorrow."

I said, "I will."

She kissed me on the forehead and said, "Good night, sweetheart."

The next morning, Kim had made breakfast, just like the good old days. I had to keep reminding myself that this wasn't the good old days. I didn't want to get caught up in something that wasn't going to happen.

When I came into the dining room, Kim said, "Good morning sleepyhead," something she used to say to me. But usually, it was followed by "I love you" and a kiss. So when she said it this time, my heart sank. She smiled at me and it felt nice having her there with me.

Kim asked, "So what time is your appointment?"

I said, "It's at one thirty"

"My mom is so excited! She keeps telling me she's going to find out the sex of her grandchild soon." Kim said.

I said, "I'm glad that makes her happy. She always makes everyone else happy, it's about time someone makes her happy."

Kim said, "Yeah, I saw all the things she bought for the baby. So are you excited about finding out the sex?"

"Well, let's just say I wasn't until your mom started talking about it all the time. Now I am. Your mother makes everything exciting" Looking at Kim her eye didn't look so god so I said. "Kim, maybe you should put something on your eye, to make the swelling go down."

Kim said, "What, you don't like my new look?" Then she started laughing and said, "Yeah, I have some cream they gave me at the hospital. I'll do it after I eat. Now let's fill you up! Grab a plate."

I wanted so badly to ask her what happened, but everything was going so well and I didn't want to mess that up. So we chatted. I washed the dishes after breakfast then went to take a shower. I got ready for my appointment, and when I came out, April was ready to go. She was acting like a kid going to Disneyland. It was great to have someone so supportive of me. I never got that growing up. I didn't have that until I met Kim, and now I was getting it from her mother.

I said, "Where's Kim? I wanted to say good-bye."

April called Kim, and when Kim came out of her room, April said, "We'll be back soon. Don't go get your stuff. I'm having the hotel send your stuff over today, so stay put until it gets here."

Kim said, "Okay, Mom, I won't go anywhere."

I said, "Good-bye, Kim."

She said, "Good-bye and good luck. I hope you get what you want." All I could think was what happened? Why didn't April want Kim to go back to the hotel? It must have something to do with her black eye. While sitting in the waiting room with April, some lady recognized her and asked for her autograph. Then the woman pulled out a camera. I took a picture of them together. A few minutes later, they called my name.

As we were going in, the nurse said only I could go in.

I said, "I want my mom in there with me."

The nurse said, "Oh, this is your mom. Well, come on in, Ms. Springs."

I guess she recognized her, too. I put my gown on then they hooked me up to some machine. I could hear the baby's heartbeat.

The doctor said, "Everything is good with the baby. I'm just a little concerned because you're having early contractions and your blood pressure is a little high. I might have to put you on bed rest soon." Then he said, "Okay, are you sure you want to know the sex of the baby? Once I tell you, there's no going back."

I looked at April, who had a big smile on her face. I said, "I'm sure."

The doctor moved the transducer on my stomach, and as we looked at the baby on the little screen, he said, "Congratulations, it's a girl."

April said, "I knew it, my first granddaughter." She was so happy and kept saying, we were going to get this and that. Then she said, "I can't wait until we get back to Los Angeles. I'm going to get my granddaughter everything she wants. I'm going to spoil her so much." April then asked the doctor how much longer it would be until I couldn't fly anymore, since we were going back to Los Angeles in three weeks.

"Well, she's close to six months along. I would say with the high blood pressure and contractions, she should get on a plane as soon as possible. I wouldn't wait three weeks. It wouldn't be good for the baby. High blood pressure and early contractions can result in an early birth."

With that said, April set a plan in motion. She declared, "You're going to have to go back soon."

We picked up some lunch, and took it back home. By the time we got there, Kim's stuff had arrived. Kim was in the living room watching TV when April said to her, "Are you hungry, babe? We brought back a late lunch."

Kim said, "Yes, I was about to make a snack." Then she asked, "How is the baby doing? What did the doctor say?"

Before I could say anything, April said, "We're having a girl."

Kim said, "Great, now you can stop bugging me about having a granddaughter for you."

April then said, "But Kim, we have a problem."

Kim sounded worried when she said, "What? Is there something wrong with the baby?"

April said, "No, the baby is fine, but the doctor says he doesn't want her to wait three weeks to get on a plane. She's having early contractions and has high blood pressure, so I have to send her back before I can leave. So that means she'll be there along with just Rosa."

Kim said, "That's not a problem. I can go back with her, until you're there in a few weeks."

April said, "Are you sure?"

Kim said, "Yes, Mom, if memory serves me right, Carrie doesn't bite."

Kim started laughing after she said that. That was the first time I heard her say my name in a long time. Kim's mom ate with us and then she went into her room to get ready for work.

While Kim and I were washing dishes, I said, "Are you sure you don't mind going back with me? I mean, I understand if you don't want to. I'll be fine by myself there; it's only a few weeks."

Kim said, "I'm going back with you, Carrie, and no, I don't mind. Wait, you didn't take up biting, did you?"

I said, "No, silly!" And we both laughed. It felt great; I had a real family again, even if it wasn't exactly how I wanted it to be with Kim. I was happy that I was spending time with her.

She said, "Um, I got a call today and someone is mad at you!"

"Oh, I forgot to call Michelle!"

She said, "Um, yeah. Why don't you call her and I'll finish the dishes."

I said, "Are you sure?"

She said, "Yes, I'm sure. If I recall correctly, you weren't all that good at washing dishes anyway."

I said, "Ha-ha, you have gotten funny in your old age!"

She said, "Since when is twenty-seven old?"

I said, "Since now!"

Then she said, "So I guess you'll be joining me in the Depends aisle next week when you turn twenty-seven! You thought I forgot, didn't you?" She started laughing.

I said, "You're so funny, Kim. NOT!"

I went into the bedroom and called Michelle. When she answered, the first thing she said was, "Well, well, well, so you do still have my number?"

I said, "I know, I know, I forgot to call you. I'm sorry. There's been a lot going on here." Michelle said, "Yeah, I heard. So is everything going okay?"

"Yes, and guess what?"

"What?"

"I'm having a girl."

Michelle said, "Well, congratulations!"

"Thanks, but the doctor says I need to hurry up and fly home. I'm having early contractions and high blood pressure. So I'm going back to Los Angeles in a few days, but April can't leave for another three weeks. So Kim is coming back with me, until April gets back."

She said, "So, you and Kim are getting along?"

"Yes, it's like I have a new friend; everything is great. So, why didn't you call me back that night? I was waiting to hear back about Kim."

Michelle said, "I spoke to April and she told me she was going to call you."

"Oh, okay. Hey, can I ask you something?"

She said, "Sure."

I said, "What happened to Kim's eye? She has a black eye."

"Yes, I know. Did you try asking her?" Michelle inquired.

"No. Things are going so well, I didn't want to upset her. When I asked April, she said I would have to ask Kim."

Michelle said, "Well, I think you need to ask her and see if she wants to tell you."

"Okay, fine. Nobody wants to tell me."

Michelle said, "If she wants you to know, she will tell you, or just ask her."

I said, "I'll think about it."

She said, "Okay, well, call me when you get back to California and I'll come up and see you."

"Okay, I will. How is everything with you and Vanessa?"

"We're getting married and you'll be getting an invitation soon. I know you're going to come, right?"

"Yes, you know I'll be there. Tell her hi for me and that I'm going to call her soon, okay?" Michelle said, "Will do."

"Okay, Michelle, take care and I'll talk to you soon."

Michelle said, "Okay, don't forget about me again!"

"I won't, I promise."

After I hung up the phone, I went into the living room where Kim was talking to her mom. She was telling Kim to book the flights and to book a car to pick us up at LAX. She also said to call Rosa and tell her to fill the house up with food and to make sure clean sheets were on the beds.

Kim said, "Okay, Mom, I got this all covered."

April said, "Thanks, Kim. You're a big help!" Then she turned to me and said, "Come sit down, sweetheart. I want to ask you something." So, I sat next to her. She said, "Have you made up your mind if you want to stay with me, or do you want to get your own place?"

"Well, if it's okay, I would like to stay with you. I'm kind of afraid to be alone with a newborn."

April said, "Of course it's okay, and it's what I wanted to hear. That means I get to turn the guest room into the baby's room. This is going to be so much fun! Have I told you how happy you have made me?"

I smiled and said, "No, you're the angel that God sent to me."

She then kissed both Kim and me and said, "I've got to get to work. Kim, don't forget to take care of those things, and you two, no biting allowed. I'll see you in the morning."

We laughed and said, "Okay, good night."

As soon as April was out the door, Kim said, "So what do you want to do?"

"I don't know, what do you want to do?"

"Well, we could start packing or we could go to the movies."

We both said, at the same time, "Go to the movies."

She said, "You look up the movies online and I'll call to book our flights, and then I'll call Rosa."

"Okay, what kind of movie do you want to see?"

Kim said, "You know what I like, stop playing."

It felt so good that we were doing things together. I know we weren't together, but I was willing to take what I could get. After I found a movie and she was done on the phone, we took a cab to the movies.

We had popcorn, Red Vines, and fruit punch. Just like the good old days. After the movies, Kim took me to get a slice of pizza.

She said, "I couldn't leave New York without having a slice of their pizza."

I had such a good time. When we got back home, we watched TV in the living room and we were being silly. We ended up falling asleep on the couch.

When we woke up in the morning, Kim said, "You're such a couch hog. I fell off twice."

I wondered why she hadn't gone to her bed, not that I wanted her to. I said, "I'm sorry, my stomach is a little bigger than usual."

April came into the living room where we were both still lying and said, "Get dressed. I'm taking my girls out to breakfast."

April took us to the Four Seasons restaurant, which was so nice. We ended up having a late lunch and honestly, I had never seen such a beautiful hotel in my life. We were all having such a good time. After breakfast, we went to Central Park to feed the birds. Next stop was Rockefeller Center. It was getting late and April had to head to work soon, so we headed home.

When we got home, I was exhausted. I was ready for bed, so I took a shower and knocked out. I didn't wake up until the next morning. I was really beginning to feel pregnant. When I went into the living room, April was there, but Kim was gone. I had no idea where she was. I didn't want to overstep my boundaries, so I didn't ask where she was. Although we were spending a lot of time together, she wasn't my girlfriend anymore. I knew I was still in love with her, but she was just being nice, and I needed to concentrate on my baby.

My mind started to wonder. Where was Kim? Did she change her mind and decide not to go back to Los Angeles with me? Did she not want to see me anymore? Then all of a sudden, she walked through the door and said, "Wow, you finally woke up. We must have worn you out yesterday. You didn't even have dinner last night; you just passed out. Have you eaten yet?"

"No, I just got up." I admitted.

"Well, look at all this food; you'd better eat. I know the baby has to be hungry." Breakfast was sitting on the table.

I said, "I'm about to." But where had she gone? Who did she go see? Did she have a special friend? Wait, what was I thinking? She had been spending all of her time with me, and I knew Kim; if she had someone special, she would be spending all her time with her. So where did she go? Okay, I had to get my mind off of this. I was going to eat breakfast and then pack my stuff so that I would be ready to go in the morning.

April said to me, "I know I'll be there in three weeks, but I'm going to miss you so much."

I said, "I'm going to miss you, too. I wish I could wait and leave with you."

Then Kim said, "Oh, I guess I'm not good enough."

I said, "No, silly, it's not that! I'm glad you're going with me and I'm grateful. It's just that all my life, I didn't really know what it was like to have a mother to care about me, let alone spend time with me, until a few months ago. You've had a wonderful mother all your life. Hey, are you willing to give your mother up?"

Kim said, "No!"

I said, "Well, neither am I. I really love your mother and I'm glad I got to know her and spent some alone time with her."

April said, "Well, I'm not giving either one of you up, so ha!"

We laughed and April hugged both of us. She said, "Awe, I'm really going to miss my girls."

When we were both finished packing, Kim said, "I have an idea. Why don't you put your shoes on. We're going out." We got a cab and pulled up to this quickie picture place. Kim had us take a picture together and had the guy put "Your girls will miss you" on the bottom of it. Then she had the guy take a picture of just my stomach and put "I'll miss you, Grandma" on it. Next we went to a frame store and got them framed. When we got home, Kim put them on her mom's nightstand.

Kim and her mom were always good together; I didn't understand why I couldn't have that kind of relationship with my mother. I mean, why did she have me if she didn't want me? It's not like I asked to be born.

Kim said, "Carrie, what do you want for lunch? I'm starving."

"You're always starving. You would think you're the one who's pregnant."

Kim grinned and said, "I know. I've been craving some weird things lately." Kim had a great figure; she could eat anything and not gain a pound. She was 5'7" and weighed about 110 pounds. I was 5'6" and weighed about 127 pounds until I got pregnant. I felt like a whale. I heard Kim calling my name. She said, "Hey, did you call Michelle and tell her we were going back to L.A. tomorrow?"

I said, "No, not yet. I mean she knows were coming back just not tomorrow"

Kim said, "Why not? You know she really misses you."

"I'll call her tonight. I'm sure she's at work right now."

Kim had no idea how bad I wanted to walk up to her and kiss her, and how much I wanted to say how sorry I was, that I never meant to betray her. I wondered if she knew how much I still loved her and wanted to be with her. I wanted this to be my family for life, but how would she ever forgive me? I mean, I was carrying around some guy's baby, a stranger at that.

"Lunch is ready," Kim said.

"Okay. Let me wash my hands and I'll be right there."

As I sat there and ate lunch with Kim, I wondered if she knew she was still the one I wanted, still the one I wanted to hold my hand, still the one I wanted to hold me at night, still the one I wanted to make love with, and still the one I wanted to share my life with. But I guessed I had blown that. After lunch, Kim brought all of our bags to the foyer, so we wouldn't have to do it in the morning. Then we sat down to watch a little TV.

All of a sudden, Kim jumped up and said, "Shit, I forgot, I have to go out! I'll be back in a few hours." Next thing I knew she was out the door, as she yelled, "Call me if you need me!"

I said, "Okay," but I couldn't ask where she was going. I had no right anymore.

I sat in front on the TV wondering where she had gone. I hated this feeling; it made me so jealous that she had a life outside of me. I remembered when I was her life. This really sucked! What was going to happen when we got back to L.A. and she did that? Would I be able to handle it? What if she started dating? Would I lose my mind? Maybe I should get my own place, so I wouldn't see that. A few hours passed and she still hadn't come back. April called to check on me.

She said, "Hi, sweetheart, I'm just calling to check on you. I know Kim had to go out for a few hours, so I wanted to make sure you were okay."

I said, "Yes, I'm fine. I'm watching TV.

She said, "Okay, I'm going on in a few minutes, so if you need me, leave me a message and I'll check it in between my scenes."

"Okay, but I'm fine. Have a great show."

She hung up and all I could think was, *Even April knew Kim was going somewhere today.* But where did she go?

Right then she walked in the door and said, "Hey, how are you feeling?"

I said, "Okay." I was thinking of asking her what happened to her eye. "Kim, why don't you get your cream and I'll put some on your eye?"

She said, "Okay."

As I was putting the cream on her eye, I said, "It's looking a lot better." It felt so good to be that close to her face. I wanted to kiss her. Then I said, "Can I ask you something?"

She said, "Let me guess. You want to know what happened to my eye?"

"Yes, I want to know who would hurt your pretty face."

She smiled when I said the pretty face part. She said, "Well, do you remember Michelle's old girlfriend, Angie?"

All I could think was *Oh my God! Had she been dating Angie? Is she the one who she has been running out to see? How could she date that girl?*

Deep in my thoughts, I heard, "Hello, Carrie, are you listening to me?"

"Sorry, yes, I am. I remember her."

She said, "Michelle took me to this party. It was a small get-together and she was trying to cheer me up. Well, Angie was there. She was a little buzzed and kept hitting on me. I kept pushing her off of me, but she wouldn't leave me alone. I got irritated when she tried to kiss me, and I told her off in front of everybody. She got mad and got some of her friends to jump me when I got to New York. So there you have it; that's how I got my black eye."

I said, "Wow, she really wants you."

Kim said, "Well, I don't want her."

I asked, "Have you been dating, or is that too personal?"

She said, "No, not really."

What did she mean by "not really"? Had she been out on dates? Did she forget me that easily, and that soon? I mean, it had only been a few months. And what was I thinking? Not only had I seen other people, but I'd slept with other people and got pregnant while still with Kim. Now I knew I would have to get my own place a few months after I had the baby. I needed to let April know. I couldn't up and move out on her. I knew how much she was looking forward to having the baby there with her. I would plan to let her keep the baby whenever she wanted. After all, she was her grandmother and a wonderful one at that. Sometimes, I thought about Kim and me raising this baby together. I knew that was selfish of me, but I could not help myself. I suddenly heard Kim say, "Why did you get so quiet?"

I said, "What?"

She repeated herself, "Why did you get so quiet?"

"Oh, I was thinking."

She said, "Thinking about what?"

I lied. I said, "Just about what I have to do when I get back to L.A."

She said, "Like what?"

I said, "You know, like setting up doctor appointments, getting stuff for the baby." Well, that saved me from telling Kim the truth.

She said, "I'll help you when we get there, don't worry."

Then I opened my big mouth and said, "You don't have to. I'm sure you have better things to do."

She said, "I'm sure I can find time for you. Don't be silly, Carrie, that's why I'm going with you, to help you. Besides, my mom will be there in three weeks. We'll work everything out."

Was she saying she would start dating once her mother got there? I was starting to lose my mind.

I got up and she said, "Where are you going?"

"I'm tired. I'm going to take a nap."

A few minutes later, Kim knocked at my door and said, "Are you sleeping?"

I said, "No, why?"

"Did I say something to upset you?"

I said, "No, the baby is wearing me out."

She said, "Are you sure?"

I said, "Yes, I'm sure." She left the room I rolled over on my side and started to cry. I was gone out of her heart; she wasn't in love with me anymore. My heart hurt so bad that it was like someone had taken all the pain in the world and put it in my heart.

She came back to my room and said, "Are you crying? What's wrong?" She hugs me.

It felt so good to feel her holding me. I didn't want her to let go. I held on so tight and cried in her arms. I started saying, "I'm sorry, I'm so sorry, I didn't mean to hurt you!"

She said, "I know, I know; it's okay. Stop crying, calm down." Then with tears in her eyes Kim said, "Look, it took me a while to realize it wasn't about me. I went to a lot of counseling and talked to my mom, and I get it now. You were hurt by what your mom did to you. I get that you were lost and didn't know which way to turn, but I'm here. I know I'm no longer your wife, but I'll always be your friend. You will always need a friend and that's what I am; a lifelong friend, no matter what."

It hurt to hear her say she was no longer my wife.

She said, "So wipe your eyes, and what do you say we get some ice cream?"

I went into the bathroom and washed my face, then went into the kitchen, where Kim was getting us some ice cream.

She hugged me again and said, "Are you okay?"

I said, "Yes."

"Good," she said, and then started squirting me with whipped cream. She kissed me on the cheek, threw me a towel, and said, "Clean yourself up, you're a mess."

We both started laughing and went into the living room with our ice cream.

Kim said, "Let's talk."

I said, "Okay." But I couldn't help but wonder what she wanted to talk about. Was she going to tell me that she met someone or that she was dating?

She said, "So now that you been out there, does this mean you like men now?"

"No, I had no idea what I was doing, but if you're asking my preference, it's women." What I really wanted to say was, "It's you!"

She said, "Oh, I see. Okay, so do you mind if I ask you a personal question?"

I said, "Well, it depends on the question."

She said, "Okay, I'll give it a shot. Did you like your first time?"

I repeated, "Did I like my first time what?"

She said, "You know, when you lost your virginity?"

I said, "Do you really want to know?"

"I asked, didn't I?"

I said, "Okay, well, the only time sex was good for me was when it was with you. There, now you know, are you happy?"

She said, "Well, yes and no!"

I said, "Okay, why no?"

She said, "No because you made love with someone other than me."

I said, "I know and like I said in my letter, if I could turn back time, none of it would have happened."

"I know that you mean that, Carrie, but it doesn't change the fact that it did happen."

I turned my head away from her; tears were coming down my face.

She said, "Carrie, turn back around." I turned around to look at her and she said, "I'm sorry. I'm not trying to make you cry." She took my hand and said, "I can see this is upsetting you. We don't have to talk about it anymore." Then, she wiped the tears from my face and said, "Let's watch something on TV that will make us laugh."

But I couldn't laugh. I only sat there and stared at the TV. I was beginning to hate my mother who made me into the monster I turned into for three months. But at the same time, I needed to take responsibility for what I had done. In life, most of the time people don't take responsibility for their actions, but I was willing to own up to what I had done. It wasn't my mother who got me drunk. It wasn't my mother who made me have sex with random people. It wasn't my mother who broke Kim's heart. It was all me. I made lots of mistakes and I was willing to own up to them. These are all the things I wanted to say to Kim, but I didn't want to bring all of her pain back.

Kim must have noticed how quiet I got because she said, "Are you all right?"

I said, "Yes, I think I'm going to bed."

She said, "It's early."

I said, "Yeah, I know, I think it's best."

"Okay, listen up, Carrie. We're about to go back to L.A. tomorrow and you are not going to be moody. Remember what I used to do to you when you got moody?" She started tickling me and I'm a very ticklish person. I was laughing when Kim said, "That's it, laugh it up, Carrie. You know you like that."

And then it happened! I kissed her, and she stopped tickling me. She kissed me back; we were caught up in the passion for the moment.

Then she stopped and said, "I don't think this is such a good idea. I'm sorry, Carrie, but I can't do this."

"What is it, Kim? Don't you love me anymore?"

She said, "No, that's it. I do love you; it's that I don't trust you. I'm afraid of you, Carrie. I don't know if you're going to break my heart again."

"I won't, Kim. I love you. You're my air, you're my heart, and I love you so much that I could never love anyone else, even if I wanted to. Please, Kim. Remember me? I'm your Carrie. I'm the one who loves you and will do anything to prove my love to you. You tell me what I need to do to show you. I miss you, I miss us, and I miss everything about us. Do you know how hard it is to sit here and not be able to touch you, kiss you, or say I love you?" I was crying as I was saying all of this to her. "I'm begging you, Kim. Please, come back to me."

She said, "I can't, Carrie. You hurt me too deeply and I don't want to go through that pain ever again. Carrie, you broke my heart and I felt like our life together was just a lie. Do you understand what you did to me? Carrie, I wanted to marry you and start a family with you. Now you're having some guy's baby you don't even know. How do you think that makes me feel?"

I couldn't say anything.

"Carrie, I was at the end of my rope when I found out you were sleeping with other people. I thought we had something special." Kim was saying this while tears were coming down her face. "I was going out of my mind the day I walked out the door. Do you know how hard it was to walk away from the woman that I loved? Carrie, we were in love for over ten years and you threw it away in a few months. You hurt me so bad that I used to pray to God every day to take my pain away. When I couldn't take the pain anymore, I ran to my mother. She didn't know what to do. She tried everything until she finally had to put me in a mental hospital."

I had no idea that Kim was that bad off. When I heard that, I started crying even more. I couldn't believe I did that to the woman I loved. How could I have done this to her? I didn't deserve her. I needed to let her go. But we were going back to L.A. together the next day.

I said, "Kim, I had no idea you were that hurt and depressed. I don't deserve you or your love, so I'm going to leave. I don't think I should be around you or your mother. I can't do this anymore. I need to go; I need to let you go be happy." As tears kept flowing down my face, I said, "I'm going to go."

Kim said, "No, you can't go. We're going to take care of you. You don't have anyone else, so why don't you go to bed and we'll go home tomorrow."

"Kim, I can't. This isn't fair to you and I can't break your heart anymore."

We were both crying and needed to get out of there.

"Kim, I really need to get out of your life, but no matter where I go or how long I live, I'll always love you." I started to get up off the floor where we ended up while we were crying. Then I went toward the door.

Kim said, "Where are you going?"

I said, "I'm going anywhere, so you don't have to deal with having me around anymore, breaking your heart."

"Carrie, you don't have anywhere to go. Besides, I don't want you to go. I want to take care of you; at least give me that part of you. Carrie, I still need you. Do you have any idea how hard it was not to run back to you? The only thing that stopped me was the pain in my heart. Now you're here. I need you here with me, even if it's just as friends. Do you want to do something for me, Carrie?"

"Anything, Kim!" I insisted.

She said, "Stay in my life. I need you in my life; if you leave you would be breaking my heart all over again." She held her arms out and I walked into them and cried. "I think we're both going to be okay."

We both slept in my bed that night. We held each other all night. That was the best sleep I had in a long time. When I woke up the next morning, Kim was still holding me. She was holding me so close, I could feel her heartbeat. She was completely knocked out. When I tried to get up without waking her, she pulled me into her like she used to do when we were together. I watched her sleep.

Then April came in and said we needed to get up or we would miss our flight. She wanted to make sure we ate breakfast before we left. She didn't say a word about us sleeping together. I think deep down inside April wanted us to be together, but she never interfered. While we were sitting at the table eating, April told Kim, "I'm counting on you to make sure Carrie eats. She will go without eating if you don't watch her and make sure she's taking her pills. Oh, and make sure she makes it to her doctor appointments."

Kim said, "I know, Mom. I'll make sure she does everything she's supposed to do. Listen, Mom, everything will be fine."

April said, "Okay, Kim, but you know I'm still going to call and check on my girls!"

Kim said, "Yes, I know, Mom."

We were all ready to go when the buzzer rang and the doorman told us our car had arrived. April rode with us to the airport. When it was time for us to go through security, April cried.

"I can't believe it's already time for my girls to leave me."

"Mom, three weeks will go by fast." Kim said; it was almost like Kim was our mom.

April hugged us and said, "I love you both," and then she watched us until she couldn't see us anymore. We went to check our tickets in and found out April upgraded us to first class.

Kim said, "I knew she was going to do that. I bet she even called Rosa to make sure I called her." After we took are seats, Kim said, "Are you comfortable?"

I said, "Yes, very."

When the flight attendant came by Kim asked if we could get some water and crackers. Then she looked to me and said, "Just in case. Why don't you take a nap?"

"Kim, I love your mom so much. I'm going to miss her."

"Yes, me too," she said. "But three weeks will fly by." Kim held my hand and said, "Don't worry; I'll take good care of you."

I said, "I know, I'm not worried about it. I just really love your mom."

Kim said, "You mean, our mom; don't let her hear you say that!"

"Hey, Kim, did she say anything to you about us sleeping together?"

Kim said, "Nope, why?"

I said, "I thought she would have said something to you about it."

"Nope, the only time my mom asks about things between us is if I look unhappy. Other than that, she lets me live. She's always there when I need her."

I said, "Your mom—oops, I mean our mom—is great; I'm going to keep her as long as I can. Do you have any idea how lucky you have been all of your life to have her as a mom?"

Kim said, "Yes, the older I get, the more I appreciate her."

We had a good flight. When we landed, Kim called our mother to let her know. A car was waiting for us at the curb after we got our luggage. When we got home, I was so tired I had to take a nap.

Chapter Fourteen

A Familiar Town, but Things

Are Not the Same

When I woke up later that evening, Kim had dinner waiting for me.

She said, "Hi, sleepyhead. How did you sleep?"

I said, "Good. Did you take a nap?"

She said, "No, I unpacked and made us dinner."

"I guess the baby is wearing me out again."

Kim replied, "You know what, we should start doing what's good for the baby."

I replied, "What, Kim?"

She said, "Walking. We should start walking."

I said, "Okay, if you think it would be good for the baby, let's do it."

Kim said, "So tomorrow we'll take the baby for her first walk. I'm so excited!"

I think Kim was excited because she felt like she was taking care of me, like she wanted to. We sat down to eat and she talked about all the things we were going to do for the baby.

"Tomorrow you need to make a doctor's appointment."

It seemed like all I was saying was, "Okay, Kim, I'll do that, Kim. Sure, Kim."

After dinner, we went into the living room to watch a movie. As soon as Kim lied down on the couch, she fell asleep. The TV and I were watching Kim.

As soon as the movie was over, I put a blanket over her and went back to my room to watch TV. When I woke up in the middle of the night, the television was off and Kim was sleeping at the foot of my bed like she was protecting me from something. I guess she'd woken up and laid there. I grabbed her and pulled her arm as she inched her way up to me, and I fell back to sleep.

When I woke up in the morning, Kim was still holding me tight, but she was fast asleep. I tried to slip out from under her, but she would pull me tighter into her. I guess after all those years of holding me, it was hard to let go. I watched her sleep and when she finally woke up, I said, "Good morning, sleepyhead."

She said, "Hey, that's my line. Why don't we eat breakfast, then you can call for your doctor's appointment and we can go for a walk afterward."

I said, "Okay."

After our walk, Kim said, "I have to go out for a while. Are you going to be okay?"

There she goes again, I thought. But where was she going? Why wouldn't she tell me? I said, "Yes, I'll be fine."

When Kim left, I took a shower and put on a shorts ensemble. It's hot in the valley today, but I wanted to lie out by the pool for a while. It was nice out there. They had a very nice pool and a Jacuzzi. I put my feet in the pool for a while, and lay out for about thirty minutes. While I was eating lunch, April called. I said, "I'm fine. Everything is good. I Spent a half hour lying out in the sun and now I'm eating lunch. Oh, Kim and I started walking today; she said it would be good for the baby, but how is it good for the baby if I'm doing all the walking?"

April laughed at my corny joke and said, "You are too funny. I can't wait to get home. I miss my girls. Kim tells me your stomach is getting big."

I was thinking *It has only been one day. Is Kim calling me fat? Do I disgust her?*

I said, "I guess. You saw me yesterday. Does it seem bigger?"

She said, "You look beautiful."

I said, "Thank you. I'm going to take a nap now. You have a good show tonight. I love you."

She said, "I love you, too. Kim is on her way home, but you call me if you need me, okay?"

I said, "Okay."

Then she said, "Good-bye, sweetheart," and hung up the phone.

I cleaned my dishes then lay down in the family room to take a nap. I wanted to know where Kim went. About fifteen minutes later, Kim walked in the door and I pretended to be asleep. She saw me and kissed me on the cheek. I could hear her in the kitchen. I guess she was making herself some lunch. I turned on the TV. She heard me and came into the family room and said, "Hey, sleepyhead, did I wake you?"

I said, "No, I was just lying here."

She said, "Why didn't you say anything when I kissed you on the cheek?"

"Because I like it when you do that. So, umm, where do you go when you have to go out?" I asked hesitantly.

She said, "Remember when I told you I got lots of counseling?"

I said, "Yes."

She said, "Well, I still go. I had to switch doctors now that we're here, so that's where I was, with my new doctor. It's still hard for me to be around you and not be able to love you the way I want to."

I looked at her. I didn't know what to say.

"Carrie, I love you and I want to be with you, but I can't get over the trust issues. So I go to deal with all of the things I'm holding inside of me; it helps me.

I started to apologize. I said, "Kim, I'm—"

But she cut me off and said, "Don't say it. I know you're sorry."

I didn't just want to be friends with Kim; I wanted to be with her. She suddenly changed the subject.

She said, "Hey, did you call Michelle to tell her that we're back in California?"

I said, "No, I forgot. I'll call her now."

Kim said, "You're too late, I knew you would forget. I spoke to her earlier. She and Vanessa are coming up for the weekend."

I said, "Great!"

Kim said, "Yeah, I figured we could have a barbecue. What do you think of that?"

"It sounds like fun. Did you know that they're getting married?"

Kim said, "Yes, Michelle told me, and they're having an engagement party in two weeks. Do you want to drive down with me for the party?"

I said, "Sure."

Kim said, "Okay, we need to go shopping for gifts soon."

I said, "Sounds great."

Then she said, "Okay, we'll go shopping tomorrow for all of the food and drinks. Does that sound like fun?"

I said, "Yes, lots of fun!"

She said, "Then next week we can go shopping for engagement presents."

"Sounds like a plan ."

"So did you eat lunch?"

"Yeah."

"Don't lie to me. Mom said you would go without eating."

I said, "You can call Mom, because she called me while I was eating."

Kim looked at me then said, "Okay, I'm going to trust you."

I said, "Wow! That's something I never thought I would hear you say."

"Ha-ha, Carrie! So what do you want to do tonight?"

"I don't know, maybe go to dinner or maybe a movie or maybe both. What do you want to do?"

Kim said, "That sounds great to me. I'm going to finish making my lunch. Why don't you go ahead and look up some movies online."

So I headed to the office and went online. Kim came in eating a sandwich, sat on the edge of the chair I was sitting in, and said, "Did you find anything good?"

I said, "No, not really. Maybe we should skip the movie."

Kim said, "I know, why don't we go to dinner and then take a walk on Venice Beach?"

I said, "Okay, but it sounds like we're going on a date." I really wished we were.

Kim said, "Let's just think of it as two old friends going to dinner and hanging out."

I was hurt when she said that, but I played it off and said, "Okay, but you can be the old friend. I'm still young."

We both laughed and Kim said, "Whatever! I'm tired; I'm going to take a nap. Do you want to take a nap with me?"

I said, "Um, what are we, like, six?" Knowing she would hold me during the nap made me want to take one with her.

Kim said, "Okay, fine!"

I said, "I'm just kidding! I need a nap too if we're going out tonight."

We took a nap on the couch and of course Kim held me the whole time. I loved it anytime I got to feel close to her. To be honest, I didn't sleep most of the time we took naps together; I would just watch her sleep. Sometimes I would trace her lips with my finger and sometimes when I did that, it awoke her. I loved her so much and could not get enough of her. Sometimes while I was in her arms, I pretended we were still together and that I was pregnant with her baby. But then reality would kick back in when she awoke and I couldn't kiss her or make love to her. I remembered when Kim and I first started sleeping together. If one of us just rolled over in bed while sleeping, we made love right then and there, and it didn't matter if we had to go to school early in the morning. I missed the good old days.

About an hour after thinking, wishing, and watching Kim sleep, I fell asleep in her arms, where I wanted to be. Kim woke me up around 7 p.m. and asked if I still wanted to go out.

I said, "Of course."

She said, "Let's get ready then."

A while later, I heard Kim yell from her room, "Are you almost ready?"

I yelled back, "I'm ready to go." But I felt like a big ol' whale.

My stomach was so big and I was getting too fat for all of the clothes that Kim's mom bought me. When Kim walked into my room, I said, "Maybe I shouldn't go out. Look at me, I'm so big I can barely fit in my clothes."

Kim said, "You look beautiful."

Every time she said something sweet to me, I felt so stupid. How could I have let her go and do the things that I did to someone who was so sweet to me? I was an idiot.

We headed out. She took me to an Italian restaurant on Melrose called Frankie's. It was a very warm family place and the food was so good. I had the lasagna and Kim had the veal. We left there and headed to the beach. We walked on the boardwalk and talked. We talked about everything—from her mom to Michelle, Vanessa, the moon, and the sun. While we were walking, Kim took my hand and held it while we talked. It was when she grabbed my hand that I noticed she wasn't wearing her wedding band. I still wore mine; I didn't have the heart to take it off. I was also still wearing the ring that

Kim bought me when she first asked me to marry her. Even though my fingers were swollen from the pregnancy, I refused to take them off.

All of a sudden, Kim said, "Look at the time; it's getting late. I need to get you home. Mom would be mad at me if she knew I had her grandbaby out this late."

I didn't want to go. I was having a great time, but Kim insisted, so off we went. All the way home, I was hoping she would sleep with me and hold me all night. Kim came in and said, "Good night," then went to sleep in her room. I wanted her in my room with me. What happened? Was she mad at me, or was she not sleeping with me anymore? I got most of my pillows and held them as if they were her. I knew that was the only way I was going to be able to sleep.

When I woke up in the morning, Kim was in my bed with me, holding me. Apparently, that was the only way she could sleep. I was so happy, knowing she still needed a part of me. It felt so good and I wasn't getting up until she awoke. When she did wake up, she said, "Hey, how did I get in here? You must have kidnapped me." She started laughing. "Come on, you need to take your pills. I'm going to make breakfast. I know if you're not hungry, the baby sure is."

I said, "I'll be down right after I wash my face and brush my teeth."

When I got down to the kitchen, Kim had my pills sitting on the counter as if to say, *First thing you do is take these pills.* So I did.

For the next few days, Kim and I spent most of our time together. It was like we were a couple again, just without the lovemaking. I noticed she had been drinking lately, and when she drank, she got very affectionate, which of course I didn't mind at all. She held my hand while we were just sitting and watching TV. Or she would rub on my stomach and kiss it. If she was on the phone, she would walk over to me and rub my back while she talked to whoever was on the phone at the time.

It was Friday. Michelle and Vanessa were coming in that day. I was so excited.

Kim said, "Let's eat and then go shopping, because I don't know what time Michelle and Vanessa are getting here."

We went to the store and it seemed like we got everything. We bought burgers, hot dogs, steaks, chips, potato salad, beans, chicken, candy, punch, —you name it, we got it. When we got home, Kim had me call Michelle to see if they were on their way.

"They're just coming over the hill. They're on the 405 and about to get off. So they will be here in about ten minutes."

Kim said, "We have good timing."

I said, "Yeah, but we're not having the barbecue until tomorrow, right?"

Kim said, "Yes, what do you think about taking them out to dinner tonight?"

I said, "It sounds good to me. Wait, am I going too?"

Kim said, "Yes, silly. Why wouldn't you? I know you don't think you're going to leave me alone with those two, do you? They're always all over each other."

I said, "Oh, wow, are they really that in love?"

Kim said, "They're both so far gone into each other. Even if Vanessa wasn't, there's no way she could get rid of Michelle. That girl is crazy about her."

Just then, we heard a knock at the door. Kim went to get it. While I put away the rest of the groceries, I heard them screaming. They must have been hugging also. Then I heard Michelle say, "Where's the mommy-to-be?"

Kim said, "In the kitchen. Go see her. Wait until you see her stomach. She looks beautiful."

It made me feel good to hear Kim say that!

When Michelle came into the kitchen, she said, "Wow, you look great! Look at the baby. Come over here and give me a hug."

After I gave Michelle a hug, I greeted Vanessa, giving her a hug as well.

Kim said, "Carrie and I thought we could take you two out to dinner tonight, since we're not having the barbecue until tomorrow."

Michelle said, "Sounds great to me." Then she looked over at Vanessa and said, "Are you okay with that, babe?"

Vanessa said, "Great, as long as I don't have to drive. How do you guys deal with all of that traffic?"

I saw what Kim was talking about. They looked so happy together. They were all over each other. They were clearly in love.

Michelle said, "Kim hasn't been bugging you, has she, Carrie? Come on, you can tell me. I hear she's making you walk now, is that true?"

"Yes, but we've only walked twice, so that's not bad."

Then Kim said, "Let's take your stuff upstairs, Michelle."

Michelle said, "Okay, where are we sleeping?"

Kim said, "In my room. It's a queen-size bed, not that you need that much room, as much as you two are all over each other."

They started laughing. Michelle kissed Vanessa before she went upstairs with Kim. They were up there for a while. They must have been talking. I was downstairs talking to Vanessa.

She said, "So are you and Kim getting along really well?"

I said, "Yeah, it's bitter sweet. We're just friends, but we do everything together. Sometimes I want to kiss her, but I can't. She tells me she still loves me, but she can't be with me right now. It's sort of funny that everything is the same, except we don't have sex. It's weird, but I'll take what I can get."

Vanessa said, "So you guys are coming up for our engagement party, aren't you?"

"Yes, I'm excited for you. Are you ready to tie the knot?"

"Yes, I'm more than ready."

"I can see that you two are so in love. When are you two actually getting married?"

"In about a year. We're having a summer wedding."

"Where are you going for your honeymoon?"

"Hawaii."

"That sounds nice! Have you two talked about having a family?"

"Yes, we want to be married at least two years before we start a family."

"How did you know she was the one?"

Vanessa stalled with her answer and then said, "Um, I'm not sure if it's okay to tell you."

I was confused and said, "Why, is it something really personal?"

She said, "No, it might upset you, though."

"I'll be fine, tell me."

"Are you sure, Carrie?"

"Yes, I'm sure!"

"Okay, it was when Michelle said, 'I love you as much as Kim loves Carrie.' " Vanessa said, "I'm sorry, but that's the truth. I used to watch you and Kim together and I knew that was what I wanted. I used to see the way Kim looked at you. She never really looked at you when she talked to you. It was like she was looking into your eyes, your soul, and your heart; she was so in love. It was like she couldn't get enough of you, or the way she always touched you or held your hand. It was like you two were one person and to me, it was so beautiful. I told myself the first time I saw you two together, *That's what I want and I won't settle for less.* You two were so in love. Like I said, it was the most beautiful relationship I had ever witnessed besides my parents."

Just then, Kim and Michelle walked back into the room. Michelle kissed Vanessa and sat beside her.

Kim said, "Okay, so where are we going for dinner? What do you two have a taste for?"

I said, "I don't really feel well. I think I'll stay here."

Kim said, "What's wrong? Does your stomach hurt? Do I need to take you to the doctor?"

"No, I'm tired."

Vanessa said, "It's my fault. I said something I shouldn't have said. I'm really sorry, Carrie."

"It's not your fault. I made you say it. Let's forget it."

Michelle said, "What happened? What did you say, babe?"

Vanessa said, "Well, she asked me how I knew you were the one for me. I told her I didn't want to tell her and she insisted, but still, I shouldn't have told her."

Michelle said, "Oh, now I get it."

Kim said, "What is it? What did she say?"

I said, "It's not your fault, Vanessa. I pushed you into telling me. I'm going to lie down. Sorry, you guys."

I went upstairs and Kim kept saying, "What did you say?" They must have told Kim because Kim came upstairs and said, "I'm sorry, Carrie. Everything is going to be okay. Besides, that's a compliment. We had something good at one time; we have to appreciate that. I mean, not many people will have what we had in their whole lifetime. I'm glad we had what we had, even if it didn't last forever. I wouldn't trade that time for anything in the world, would you?"

Now I knew that Kim would have taken the dance. I replied to her question with a firm "No!"

She said, "Okay, then, you should be happy someone wants what we had. Now, where's my smile?"

I smiled and Kim kissed me on the cheek and said, "Let's go, okay?"

I smiled and said, "Okay."

Then she said, "I hope you know I'm sleeping with you while they're here because I put them in my room."

I was so happy that I didn't have to guess if she was going to sleep with me while they were here.

I went downstairs and Vanessa said, "I'm really sorry. I didn't mean to upset you!"

I hugged her and said, "I know; it's okay."

Then we left to go eat. We had lots of fun at dinner and they told us how they had gone to some party where they ran into Angie, and she looked like someone had whipped her ass. It turned out she tried to play some girl, and the girl beat the shit out of her. Angie was such a loser. Then they told us all these stories about when their parents came down, once they found out they were engaged, and how Michelle's brother was trying to pick up on women at a lesbian bar they took him to. We were just laughing and laughing. At one point, Kim started holding my hand under the table. It felt nice. I think seeing Michelle and Vanessa being all over each other made her miss what we used to have.

When we got back, Michelle and Vanessa were in their room getting ready for bed. The door was cracked. I heard Vanessa saying, "This is crazy; they're clearly still in love with each other. You can see it in their eyes. Why don't they get back together?"

Michelle said, "Leave it alone, babe. It's none of our business."

"Yes, but Michelle, they don't just love each other; they're both still in love with each other. Did you see the way they look at each other?"

Kim walked up behind me and scared me. She said, "What are you doing?"

I played it off and said, "Nothing. I was going to go make sure they had enough blankets."

Kim said, "That will be the least of their problems, as much as they're all over each other. I'm just glad we have thick walls." We both laughed and then Kim said, "Come on, let's go to bed."

By the time I changed, Kim was already in the bed. She said, "Hurry up, I'm sleepy and you know I need my bed warmer."

When I crawled into bed, Kim pulled me into her and kissed my forehead. All I could think was, *Why can't that kiss be on my lips?* But then I laid my head down and went to sleep in Kim's arms.

The next day, Kim woke up bright-eyed and bushy-tailed. She started waking me up with kisses all over my face, but none of the kisses were on my lips.

She said, "Get up, sleepyhead. We're having a barbecue today. We have company!" She was in such a good mood.

We got up, washed our faces, and brushed our teeth. As we were passing by the room Michelle and Vanessa were in, we heard them fooling around.

Kim said, "Damn, do they ever stop?" We started laughing.

Just as we were done making breakfast, April called and asked Kim if I made my doctor's appointment. Kim told her to hold on and shouted, "Carrie, did you make your appointment?"

"Yes, I did. It's Monday at two p.m."

After speaking to Kim, she asked to speak to me. "Good morning, sweetheart. How are you feeling?"

I replied, "I'm good, except one thing."

She said, "What is it? Does your stomach hurt?"

"No, it's just that I miss you."

"Oh silly, I miss you too. I'll be home soon enough, try to hang in there. Is Kim taking good care of you?"

"Yes, she's doing a great job."

"Good, I'm glad to hear that. Well, I love you and I'll talk to you soon."

"I love you too."

She asked to speak to Kim again for a minute. I handed Kim the phone and Kim said, "Okay" to whatever her mom asked of her, then she hung up and said, "Carrie, come here."

So I walked over to Kim, she bent down and kissed my stomach. She said, "Mom wanted me to kiss her grandbaby for her."

I thought that was so cute.

Then Kim said, "I'm going upstairs to get them to come down and have breakfast. Wish me luck," and we laughed. When Kim came down she said, "Breakfast might turn into brunch with those two, my goodness! Before I knocked at their door, I could hear them still fooling around."

I said, "Did you tell them to come eat?"

Kim said, "Yeah, they knew I heard them. I could hear them laughing after I knocked. They said they were coming. I'm so glad Michelle finally found someone to be happy with."

"Yeah, me too."

Michelle and Vanessa came into the dining room. We all held hands around the table and said grace. Then Kim got up, went into the kitchen, came back with my pills, and said, "Take these first, Carrie. You thought I forgot."

I took my pills and we all ate.

Kim said, "We thought we'd take you guys down to Hollywood Boulevard. We can take some pictures, go to some shops, then come back and have a barbecue. How does that sound to you?"

Michelle said, "Sounds like fun. What do you think, babe?"

Vanessa said, "As long as I'm with you, it all sounds like fun."

Kim and I said, "Aw, how sweet," in a teasing voice.

They were in love and it was bittersweet. I was happy for them, but it was also a reminder of how Kim and I used to be.

Michelle said, "Hey, Carrie, your birthday is next week. What are your plans?"

"I don't really have any. I'm kind of getting depressed thinking about it. I'm going to be old like Kim!" We all started laughing. When I was laughing, I felt the baby kick for the first time.

I said, "Wow!" and grabbed my stomach.

In a panic, Kim said, "What's wrong?"

I said, "Nothing, I just felt the baby kick for the first time."

Kim jumped up out of her seat, held my stomach, and said, "I want to feel it." Then she felt it, a tear forming in her eye. She said, "Oh my God, I have to call my mother." She got April on the phone and said, "Mom, the baby just kicked for the first time, I felt it." She had tears coming down her face while she was telling her mom.

I overheard Vanessa whisper to Michelle, "You see, that's Kim's baby."

Michelle said, "Stay out of it, let them do their thing."

Vanessa said, "But babe, look at her. She's so excited about the baby, as if it's hers."

When Michelle looked at Vanessa, she noticed that Vanessa had tears coming down her face. I guess it was all too sad for her. Michelle grabbed Vanessa's hand and said, "We'll be right back." They went into the bathroom and Michelle calmed her down. When they came back in to finish breakfast, her tears were gone. Kim hung up the phone and wiped her tears.

For the rest of the day, Kim kept feeling my stomach, just in case the baby kicked. Every time she did, I would see Vanessa give Michelle that look, like *This is crazy*. After a day in Hollywood, we got back to the house and I was exhausted.

I told Kim I needed a nap. Kim said, "Okay, you go lie down and we'll get the barbecue started. When you wake up, you can eat, but take your pills first."

I said, "Okay, I'll do that now."

Michelle said, "I think we need a nap first too!"

Kim said, "Oh no, you don't! Michelle, don't even try it." Kim handed Michelle a drink and said, "Come on, let's get this started. Besides, I want to hear all about your wedding plans."

I headed upstairs. I must have really been tired, because it seemed like as soon as I hit the pillow, I was out like a light. I was awakened a while later, when I felt Kim rubbing and kissing my stomach.

She said, "Wake up, sleepyhead. You must have been really tired. You have been sleeping for at least three hours."

I said, "Yeah, where are Michelle and Vanessa?"

"They have been in the bathroom for about twenty minutes!" We both started laughing. "I want you to get up and eat."

I wondered how much Kim had to drink. She seemed a little buzzed. When she pulled me up, she kind of stumbled.

I said, "Are you okay?"

She said, "Yes," and started to laugh.

I said, "Let me wash my face, then I'll be down."

She said, "Okay, don't take too long because I miss you when you're not around."

At that point, I knew she had been drinking. You know what they say: When you drink, the truth comes to light. When I came downstairs, they were all kind of buzzed.

Michelle grabbed me and said, "You look so cute pregnant." Then she rubbed my stomach and said, "I can't wait until my baby gets pregnant."

Kim said, "I know, doesn't she make a beautiful pregnant woman?"

Vanessa said in a slur, "I bet she would make a beautiful bride too."

And Michelle said, "Babe, don't start."

The more Vanessa drank, the more she talked. At one point, she started crying and let everything come out. She was talking to Michelle like we weren't there. She said, "No, babe, this is crazy! They are still in love. Why can't they be together? This is breaking my heart. Look at them, just look. Why can't that be Kim's baby and they live happily ever after? Tell me, babe, tell me?"

Michelle said, "Calm down, it's going to be okay. You need to get yourself together."

Vanessa said, "What is there to get together? They're still in love and Carrie knows what she did was wrong. She's been paying for her mistakes for months."

Michelle took Vanessa to the bathroom to calm her down again. Kim and I stood there, not knowing what to say.

Finally, Kim said, "She'll be all right." And then Kim got another drink. I was the only sober person. *I might just be the only one who remembers this night,* I thought.

When they came out of the bathroom, Michelle said, "She's fine now, I'm sorry, you guys."

Then everybody started acting silly. We all sat down at the table in the backyard to eat. While we were eating, Kim's hands were all over me. She said it, without missing a step. "I love you."

I didn't say anything. I let her be drunk and say and do what she wanted. She kept kissing me on my cheek. At one point, she kissed my lips, something I had been wanting for a long time. But I wasn't sure if she knew that she had kissed my lips. I don't think Michelle and Vanessa saw her do it; they were too busy being all over each other.

I got up to get some water out of the kitchen and Kim asked, "Where are you going?"

I said, "To get some water."

Kim said, "I'll get it for you, babe."

I was shocked. Wow, she called me babe.

"No, you're drunk. I'll get it; it's okay." I went into the kitchen to get the water. I opened the refrigerator and when I turned back around, Kim was right behind me. She pinned me up against the refrigerator and started kissing me very passionately. I was kissing her back, but then I stopped. I said, "Kim, you're drunk, and you really don't want to do this."

Kim said, "I do want to do this. Do you know how hard it is for me to not be able to touch you and make love to you? I want you so bad. Let's go upstairs and make love, please, Carrie."

I wanted her so badly, but not like this.

"Kim, we can't do this while you're drunk. I want you to know what you're doing, and it's not right; you're in the wrong mind-set!"

She started kissing me and saying, "Don't you want me anymore, Carrie?"

"Yes, Kim, I want you more than you know. But not like this, it's not right."

She said, "Babe, I need you right now. I want to make love to you; let me make you feel good. My body craves you, please!"

I said, "Kim, if you still want me when you're sober, you can do whatever you want to me."

She said, "You promise?"

I said, "Yes, now let's go back outside and have fun."

When we went back outside, Michelle and Vanessa were slow dancing to the music playing.

Kim said, "At least dance with me."

Then Kim held me close and we danced. It was nice. The sun had set and the light in the backyard was beaming onto the pool. It was very romantic. We were so into each other that we didn't even notice that Michelle and Vanessa had made a clean break to their room to take one of their special naps.

"Kim, why don't you go lie down and I'll clean up. You're drunk and I think you should sleep it off."

Kim said, "No, I'll help you."

"No, Kim, go lie down. I can do it. I'm the only sober one here."

Kim said, "I'm not ready to go to sleep." Then she got another drink, sat down, and said, "Carrie, come here and sit with me."

So, I did. Kim was so drunk. She rubbed my stomach and said, "You know, this is my baby, this is my little girl inside of you. I always wanted a family with you."

I said, "Okay, whatever you say, Kim."

Then Kim got mad and said, "Are you saying this is not my baby?"

I said, "No, I didn't say that, Kim. You need to go lie down." I took her drink and said, "You're not drinking anymore."

I started cleaning up and she kept following me around saying things like, "What are we going to name our baby?" and "I think we should get married before the baby is born," and "We need to buy a house with a backyard, so the baby can play in the backyard."

I kept cleaning and saying, "Okay, Kim," to anything she said. I knew she was saying it because she was drunk.

Then she said, "I'm calling my mother, and I'm telling her we're getting married."

I had to grab the phone from her and say, "No, Kim, don't do that."

Then she went into this rant saying, "Oh, you're not going to marry me? So you're going to break my heart again? Answer me, Carrie." And then she started crying.

I felt so bad. I said, "Don't cry, Kim, you know I'll marry you. But if you don't feel the same way when you're sober, I don't think you should call your mother and tell her. Kim, listen to me; let's see how you feel in the morning, okay?"

She said, "Carrie, you don't understand. I love you and I'm still in love with you. I never stopped loving you and I want to be with you. All I want to do is spend my life with you. I want to raise our baby together and we should have one more. Don't you want that?"

"Of course I do, but not like this, Kim. Why don't you go lie down?"

"I don't want to lie down unless you're coming with me and we're going to make love." Then she started pulling on me and kissing me, saying, "Come on, baby, let's go make love. I need to touch you, I need to taste you; it's been so long, Carrie. Let me make you feel good. Do you remember when I used to make love to you?"

I said, "Kim, please stop, don't do this."

Then she started yelling, "Oh, what, you don't want me? You want a man, is that it?"

I started crying. She was starting to hurt my feelings and she was getting loud.

Michelle and Vanessa came running down the stairs and tried to get Kim to stop, but Kim said, "Go back upstairs, this is none of your business."

Vanessa said, "Come on, Carrie, come with me."

Kim said, "Vanessa, what are you doing? You know Carrie and I belong together. You said it yourself."

Vanessa said, "Yes, Kim, you do, but not like this."

I went with Vanessa, and then Kim started throwing things. I could hear Kim and Michelle as we were walking away. "Calm down, Kim, everything is going to be okay."

Vanessa took me in my room and asked me what happened. I told her and she said, "Oh, she's drunk, so the truth is coming out of her."

Still crying, I said, "Yes, but I need her to say these things to me when she's sober, Vanessa. When she's sober, she says she can't be with me because she doesn't trust me and I don't know what to do! I've never seen Kim this way. I've never seen her throw and break things. I'm starting to think maybe I shouldn't be here with her. I love her, but I don't want to hurt her any more than I already have."

A few minutes later, Michelle came in the room and said, "She's passed out on the couch. Carrie, you know these are all the things she goes to counseling for, right? I told you a long time ago she would not know how to trust you, do you remember?"

I said, "Yes."

"Carrie, I'm thinking that maybe when April comes back, Kim should come down to San Diego and hang out with us for a few days."

"Whatever helps her, I'm fine with."

Michelle then said, "Of course, you two are coming down for the engagement party."

"I'm not sure I should come. Maybe it would be better if she went alone; you know she needs some space."

"I really don't think she's going to leave you here by yourself."

"I'll mention it to her and see what she says."

"Oh, and don't worry, I cleaned up the glasses that she broke."

I went downstairs to make sure Kim had a blanket on her, and then returned to clean up the rest of the mess from the barbecue. When I was done, I kissed Kim on the cheek and headed to bed. It really sucked that Kim wasn't sleeping with me that night, but I guess it was the end of the road for that. While lying in bed, I could hear Michelle and Vanessa fooling around. All I could think was *I remember when that was Kim and me.* Was this going to happen every time I heard someone making love or kissing, or when I saw someone holding hands with their lover? Would I always think and remember when that was Kim and me? I guess it was better to have some memories than no memories at all.

I fell asleep about an hour after I laid down. When I woke up in the morning, I heard Michelle and Vanessa fooling around again. My goodness, did they ever come up for air? After I got myself together, I headed downstairs to make breakfast for everyone. But as I got closer to the kitchen, I smelled food cooking. When I went into the kitchen, Kim was in there holding her head and trying to cook. I said, "What's wrong, do you have a hangover?"

"Oh my God, Carrie, my head is killing me."

"Did you take anything?"

"Yes, but it hasn't kicked in yet."

"Okay, go lie down, Kim, and I'll finish breakfast."

"Okay." I knew Kim's head must have really been hurting for her to let me finish the cooking. She knew I wasn't that good at it and whenever she could avoid having me cook, she did. I did my best then called the girls down to eat. Of course everybody ate, but I don't think it was that good. Kim was trying to eat when all of a sudden, she ran to the bathroom to throw up. She was really hung over.

Michelle said, "Why don't we stay here and lay around by the pool, maybe go swimming, since Kim is hung over? I mean, we're leaving tonight anyway."

I said, "Okay, I'm going to go check on Kim. I'll be right back."

When I got to the bathroom, Kim was slugged over the toilet and looked bad. I called Michelle in to help me get her up. I told Kim to take a shower because it might help make her feel better. Michelle, Vanessa, and I all got ready and lay out by the pool.

When Kim got out of the shower, she came out and said, "I'm going to lie down for a while."

When lunchtime came, I played it safe and ordered some pizza.

Michelle said, "I'm going to go check on Kim."

I said, "Okay."

When Michelle came back down, she said, "Kim is feeling better, but Carrie, she doesn't remember most of last night. I'm just giving you a heads up."

I said, "Okay, then I'm not going to bring it up."

When Kim walked out, she said, "Does anyone want some wine?"

Everyone at the same time said, "No!"

Kim looked at us and said, "Okay," as she went back inside. Then, she came back with a glass of wine in her hand.

I walked up to her and took it. "What are you doing? Kim, you have a hangover; you really don't need that."

She said, "The best thing for a hangover is to have another drink."

"Kim, can you do this for me, please? I don't want you to drink today, please."

"Okay, Carrie, for you." She drank some juice instead. We all looked at one another. Kim laid down in one of the chairs next to me and said, "I should jump in the pool with all my clothes on."

Michelle said, "I dare you!"

So Kim got up and looked at the pool, and then Michelle pushed her in. Michelle had already been swimming and jumped in right behind her. They were having a good ol' time. Vanessa, who was sitting next to me in one of the chairs, asked me if I was going to say anything to Kim about what happened last night.

"No, I don't think that's such a good idea."

Vanessa said, "I'm sorry about what I said last night. I meant every word I said, but it's not my place to say anything."

"It's okay, I understand." I hugged her and said, "I know we're all going to be friends for a long time and shit will happen, so don't worry about it. Everything will be just fine."

About two hours later, Michelle got out of the pool and said, "Hey, babe, we need to get ready to go."

Vanessa said, "Okay, why don't you get in the shower. I'll pack our stuff and get you something to wear."

Michelle said, "It's not that simple."

Vanessa asked, "Why not, babe?"

Michelle said, "I need someone to wash my back!"

Vanessa smiled bit her bottom lip and said, "I think I can do that."

Kim asked, "Do you two ever stop?"

Michelle replied, "Why should we?"

Kim said, "Good point!"

Then they headed inside.

Kim said, "So, Carrie, what do you want to do tonight?"

"It's been such a long day, Kim, and I have my doctor's appointment tomorrow. I thought maybe a little TV first, and then I'm going to turn in early. I want to be well rested when I see the doctor."

Kim said, "Okay, maybe that's a good idea since I'm trying to get over this hangover."

I started cleaning up the mess around the pool when Kim came over to me and asked, "How are you feeling?"

I said, "I'm okay. How are you feeling? I mean is your head any better?"

"Yes, finally. I haven't had a hangover like that since the night we graduated and went to all those parties. Do you remember that?"

"Yes, we were both hurting that day!"

Michelle and Vanessa came downstairs with all of their stuff, ready to go. We walked them out and gave them hugs good-bye. After they drove away, Kim and I went back inside. Kim and I watched a little TV, and then I got up and said, "I'm going to bed."

Kim said, "I'll go with you."

"No, you'd better sleep in your bed."

She looked at me and said, "Did I do something wrong?"

"No, I want to sleep alone tonight."

She looked at me kind of funny and said, "Okay."

I really wanted her to sleep with me, but after watching her hurt last night when she was drunk, I didn't think it was a good idea if we slept together anymore. I didn't want Kim to hurt over me anymore. When I was lying in bed, all I could think was that I was being selfish having Kim with me all the time. I wanted my life to be all about Kim, but I had a baby to think about. I thought it was time to give Kim her space.

The next morning came and Kim was up before me. She had made breakfast, had my pills sitting on the counter, but she was very quiet. When I said, "Good morning," all she said was, "Hi," not "Good morning, sleepyhead," as she always would. Then she set a plate in front of me at the table and said, "I hope you like it."

I said, "You know I love your cooking," and she replied "Okay, good."

I knew she was mad at me because I wouldn't let her sleep with me. She didn't talk much during breakfast, and when she was done, she said, "I have to go out. I'll be back around one. Be ready to go to your doctor's appointment."

I said, "Okay," and she left—no kiss on the cheek or forehead. This really sucked! I called Michelle and told her happened and how Kim was acting.

Michelle said, "She's hurt that you didn't let her sleep with you."

I said, "I know, that's what I'm trying to avoid, hurting her!"

Michelle said, "Carrie, you're going to have to give her some time."

"I know, I just don't like to see Kim unhappy."

She said, "Well, where is she now?"

I said, "She went out."

Michelle said, "Oh, she went to her session."

"Oh, so you know about that?"

Michelle said, "Yes, and she told me you know now, so it's okay to say something about it."

"Yeah, I felt so bad when she told me she had been in a mental institution."

"Yes, but it helped her a lot. She was only in there for three weeks, but I know it really helped her. You know Kim still loves you and I don't think that will ever change."

"Yes, I know she loves me and I love her, but if my love hurts her, then I'm willing to let her go. I think I'm going to talk to April about getting my own place. Maybe that will help Kim."

"I don't know, Carrie. That might hurt April if you move out. Maybe I can talk Kim into moving back down here."

"If you think that would help her, then I'd say okay, but I'm going to miss her. Can I tell you something Michelle?"

"Sure."

"You know it's going to kill me when she finds someone new."

"I know, and I'll be there for you."

I asked, "How are you going to do that when you're always busy doing it with Vanessa?"

She started laughing and said, "I'll make the time for you. You know that Vanessa and I care about you. You're the little sister I never had"

"I know, I'm just kidding. Anyway, I think as soon as April gets back, you should have Kim come spend some time with you guys. Take her out and see if you can get her to have some fun, instead of worrying about me all the time."

Michelle said, "Can I tell you something, Carrie?"

I said, "Sure."

"If I had my way, you and Kim would get back together and live happily ever after. I still believe in my heart that will happen one day. Maybe not tomorrow, or even next week. It may be ten or twenty years from now, but someday you two will get back together, the way it's supposed to be."

"I wish I could believe that, but as of right now, I need to let her go to be happy. That's how much I love her!"

"That's fine, but I'm not going to help her find someone new and you know Vanessa is definitely not going to do that."

"I don't think anyone has to help Kim find someone new. You know how girls flock to her." Starting to feel sad thinking about Kim with someone else, I said, "Well, I'm going to go get ready for my doctor's appointment now. I'll talk to you soon."

She said, "Okay, Carrie. Call me if you need to. Bye."

I said, "Okay, tell Vanessa hi for me."

She said, "Will do."

I said, "Good-bye."

I went upstairs to take a shower and get dressed. I didn't put that much makeup on because it was really hot outside. I went down to the kitchen and made Kim and I some lunch; sandwiches, something I knew she could eat that I made. When Kim got back, she asked if I was ready to go. I told her we had plenty of time and that I had made us lunch, but she didn't seem to want it.

I said, "Aren't you going to eat your lunch I made for you?"

She said, "No, I'm not hungry, but thanks." She said it in kind of a cold voice.

I guessed she was still mad at me, so I ate my lunch and we headed to the doctor. While we were driving, I tried to talk to Kim, but everything I said to her was answered back with "yes" or "no," or "I don't know." So I didn't say anything the rest of the way. When the doctor called me in, Kim didn't get up, so I said, "Are you coming?"

She said, "I didn't think you wanted me to!"

"Of course I want you to come in with me."

"Okay, then, I'll come in."

When I started taking my clothes off to put on my gown, Kim turned around as if she didn't want to see me naked. She really was starting to hurt my feelings, but I still didn't say anything, I just took it. When the doctor came in, Kim sat there not saying anything. The doctor did a blood test and a sonogram. Then he said, "Your blood pressure is a little high."

I asked, "What do I need to do?"

"Relax and stay calm."

He asked me to set my next appointment, which would be in two weeks. I got dressed and we headed home, again, with Kim still not speaking. So I asked her, "Is there something wrong?"

"No, everything is fine!" Again, she was cold.

I said, "Kim, why aren't you talking to me?"

She said, "I answered you, didn't I?"

I was stunned. All I could say was "Wow! Well, my next appointment isn't for another two weeks and your mom will be back by then. Why don't you go down to San Diego and hang out with Michelle and Vanessa for a while?"

She said, "Because I can't leave you by yourself!"

"You heard the doctor, everything is fine. I'll be okay by myself."

"No, he said your blood pressure is high."

"No, he said it's a little high."

"Like I said, I can't leave you by yourself. My mom would kill me!"

"Oh, so the reason you're here is because your mom wants you here? I don't need you. Why don't you go? I could use some time to myself!"

Kim got really mad and said, "Oh, you don't need me? Okay, fine!" She got loud, then pulled her cell phone out, called Michelle, and said, "I'm coming down, I'll be there in about three hours," then she hung up the phone. My cell phone rang after that; it was Michelle.

She said, "What's going on? Is April back?"

"No, Kim needs to be down there."

She asked, "Why, Carrie?"

I said, "I'll call you back."

As we pulled up to the house, Kim jumped out of the car and slammed her door. She came to my side of the car and helped me out. Then she said, "I see you need me to help you out of the car." I tried to tell her that I didn't mean it like that, but she was walking so fast and so far ahead of me. Once I got to the front door where she was holding it open for me, I said, "Kim, calm down. What is wrong with you?"

She said, "Nothing, I'm going to go pack."

I said, "Kim, please!"

"Kim, please what? You told me to leave, so I'm leaving."

"Look, Kim, I just think you need some time away from me. You're not very happy with me, so take some time for yourself."

She said, "Okay, so I'm going to pack. What's the problem?" Kim packed and said, "Later!" Then she left.

I called Michelle back. "Hey, Michelle."

She immediately said, "Okay, Carrie, what's going on?"

"Well, when Kim got home from her appointment, she was very standoffish, and then she started saying things to hurt my feelings."

After I told Michelle everything, she said, "Carrie, you know she's hurting from not being able to sleep with you last night."

I said, "I know, Michelle, but it's in her best interest. Well, anyway, she's on her way down."

Michelle said, "Okay, I'll talk to her when she gets here."

"Michelle, I'm trying to do the right thing. I know Kim deserves someone special, but she's not going to get that hanging around me. I mean, what's the point if she's not going to be with me?"

"I'm going to talk to her when she gets here."

I said, "Okay, I'll talk to you later. Good-bye, Michelle."

She said, "Carrie, try to cheer up, okay?"

I didn't answer her.

I heard, "Carrie? Carrie?"

I said, "Okay, I'll try, but I don't know how much longer I can do this."

She said, "It will be okay, Carrie. I'll call you later. Bye."

I started to think maybe I should get in my car and leave, but where would I go? My mother was nowhere to be found, and if she saw me pregnant, that would give her another reason to hate me, especially since I didn't have a husband. Then I thought about how it would hurt April, and that's the last thing I wanted to do. I turned on some music and thought about when Kim and I went out for the first time in San Diego. We took a long walk at Mission Beach. We took our shoes off and walked in the water. It was so much fun. It was one of those nights where the full moonlight beamed across the water as we were holding hands. I remembered that she stopped me, kissed me, looked into my eyes and said, "I'll never leave you. We're going to spend our lives together and it will be a good life. People will try to tear us apart and I'll do my best not to let that happen. I hope you do the same. If it gets hard, I'll look back on this night and remember what I said to you, and honor my wishes. If someone takes you away from me, I'll love you from a distance. If you fall out of love with me, I'll remember the days that you did love me, just so I can always have your heart. And if it all works out and we're together for life, when I die, I want to die in your arms, so that you'll always remember me holding you. That's how much I love you, Carrie."

Tears filled my eyes when she said all this, thinking this was something she had read somewhere. I asked, "Who wrote that?"

She simply said, "My heart."

That's how I knew I needed this woman for the rest of my life. I loved her soul and her spirit; I loved Kim. It was as if God sent her down to me and said, "Carrie, this soul is for you, there is only one heart between you and that's all you'll need." This woman could move heaven and earth as far as I was concerned. She always made me feel like dancing. It was like having every dream I ever wanted come true. Now I was missing her and I was giving her away. How could anyone give something so beautiful away?

My heart was saying,

I love you, Kim with all my heart. Come back to me. I'll never hurt you again. I'll protect your heart like it's my own. I'll smother you with kisses. I'll hold you in my arms. I'll make love to you and show you that my body is yours and only yours. I'll not look, touch, or even think about loving another the way I love you. I want to go back to our world, the one that God created for us. Come dance with me forever, hold my hand, kiss my lips, and look into my eyes. I'm still here and I'm still yours. Let me make you smile again and let me make your heart feel good again. I want to wake up every morning to your face. I want to feel your body next to me every night and every morning.

All I knew was that I loved Kim and wanted to be with her, but she could not be with me. So I had to let her go, no matter how I felt. I didn't understand sometimes why we don't get a second chance at the same things, if we learned from them. Shouldn't things work out after that? Why do we always have to lose the ones we love? I know we're not supposed to question God, but when someone's heart is hurting this bad, I wanted to understand. Is that so bad?

I was getting sleepy, so I turned the music off and went to sleep. The next day, I made myself some breakfast and took my pills. After breakfast, I took a shower then decided to lie out. I found myself missing Kim again. While I was lying out, I heard the doorbell ringing. When I opened the door, I saw a woman. She was about 5'9", she had dark brown hair, and she was very pretty.

"Hi, is Kim here? Kim Springs?"

"No, she's out of town. Can I give her a message for you?"

"Do you know when she's coming back?"

"I'm not sure, but I can call her and give her a message."

"Sure, can you give her my number and ask her to call me? I'm an old friend and I would love to see her. I have been looking for her for years. I believe we have some unfinished business; she'll know. Here's my card. Thank you!"

I said, "You're very welcome. Have a good day."

As I walked back into the house, I looked at the card and my heart dropped. It said, "Camie James." This was Kim's first girlfriend, her first love. This was the girl who had her heart. This was the girl that Kim was so in love with. She was so in love with her, she even got a tattoo on her arm that said C.J. This was the one who got away. I was at a crossroad. I didn't know if I should call Kim to tell her that the love of her life was looking for her.

Chapter 15

Good-bye, My Love

I was scared I was I about to lose Kim forever. I picked up the phone and called Michelle, but she didn't answer, so I left her a message. Then my phone rang. It was April.

"Hi, sweetheart, how are you?"

I said, "I'm okay. How are things going out there?"

She said, "They're good, although I'm ready to come home."

I said, "Yeah, I'm ready for you to come home too!"

She said, "So, how did it go at the doctor's?"

"It went fine. He said everything looks good and that we're right on schedule." I didn't want to worry her about the high blood pressure.

She said, "Well, good. Have you been taking your pills?"

"Yes, I take them in the morning and in the afternoon." As I was sitting there on the phone with April, I pondered if I should tell her who came by, but I was afraid. Then I told myself, why worry April?

She asked, "Can I speak to Kim?"

"She's not here right now."

"Okay, I'll call her on her cell phone. I guess I'll talk to you soon. I love you."

"I love you, too, and can't wait until you get home."

About ten minutes later, my phone rang, it was Kim, she was yelling at me. "Why did you tell my mom I wasn't there?"

"Kim, I said you're not here right now."

She said, "Stop, you're lying. I'm tired of your shit! All you do is lie to me now, and you want me to trust you? Have you lost your mind?"

She kept yelling at me. I couldn't get a word in edgewise. "Kim? Kim? Kim?" I called out to her.

But she said, "I don't want to talk to you, Carrie. You're nothing but a big liar!" Then she hung up on me.

I tried to call her back, but she wouldn't answer. I decided I wouldn't tell her mom anything. How did we get here? Now, I was a big liar? *Wow!* I thought. *She is really pissed.* And that was what I didn't want to happen. She'd started to resent me.

Michelle called me back and said, "Kim is really pissed at you right now. I'm trying to calm her down, but she's about to come home."

"Michelle, I didn't tell her mother that she left me. April asked to speak to her and I said she's not here right now. Then, she said ok, 'I'll call her on her cell phone.' Michelle, I promise that's it. Why is she so angry with me?"

Michelle said, "She's hurt and upset with you right now. You know we tried to take her out, but she wouldn't go. She's been walking around here hurt. Carrie, here's what you need to do when she gets home. Ask her if you can talk to her, and then tell her why you didn't want her to sleep with you anymore. Be honest with her. She thinks you're being hurtful, and that you don't love her anymore. Tell her about the night she got drunk, you have to."

I said, "Yeah, well that's the least of my problems. This morning, her old girlfriend came by looking for her."

Michelle was surprised and said, "What old girlfriend? I've never heard of any old girlfriend."

I said, "You know that tattoo she has on her arm, C.J.?"

Michelle said, "Yes!"

"Well, that was her first girlfriend. When they were young, C.J.'s mom walked in on them kissing, so they sent her away to school."

Michelle said, "What?"

"Yes, and Kim was heartbroken. Now C.J. is looking for her. She asked me to have Kim call her and said they have some unfinished business."

Michelle said, "Wow, Carrie!"

"Yeah, and I don't want to tell her because I know I would lose her forever!"

Michelle said, "Carrie, you can't keep that from her."

"I know, but that doesn't change the fact that I don't want to tell her."

"Look, I know that Kim loves you. That's not going to disappear overnight."

"No, but maybe she never really stopped loving C.J. I mean, if she's looking for Kim, maybe Kim still wants her too."

Michelle said, "How did she find Kim?"

"I don't know, maybe through her mother's name."

"Yeah, but she had to have been with Kim in Arizona. Kim had been living there since she was a baby, then she came to Los Angeles and met you. You know, Carrie, this is getting crazy."

"I know, Michelle!"

Michelle said, "Well, she's about to leave, and I want to talk to her before she leaves. So, I'll have to call you back."

I said, "Okay, good-bye, Michelle."

"Bye," she said, then hung up.

I knew since I had brought up the whole C.J. thing, I was going to have to tell Kim. I sat there. I knew it was time that I moved out and that I couldn't deal with this. I would be stressing out and I couldn't afford to do that with my baby in my stomach. I was getting nervous; I didn't know what was going to happen when Kim got home. I'd never seen her like this. I was thinking I should have let her sleep with me. This whole ordeal was wearing me out. I took another shower to try to wash the stress off, but that didn't help. So I lay down for a while. I fell asleep and when I awoke, it was two hours later. I felt like I had the whole world on my shoulders. Then my stomach started to hurt, so I called the doctor. He told me to come in and see him.

I jumped in my car and headed to the doctor. When I got there, he took some tests and told me my blood pressure was too high. I told him I was stressed out. Of course he advised me I needed to calm down. He admitted me into the hospital. After about four hours of lying in the hospital bed, my phone rang. It was Kim.

I said, "Hello," then she quickly started yelling at me again.

"Where are you? I came back to take care of you like my mother asked me to do and you're not even here! I've been here for about two hours. What, are you out with one of your boyfriends?"

"Kim, please stop yelling at me, I can't do this."

She said, "What, are you afraid? He's going to hear me? Okay fine, Carrie! Do what you want to do!" She hung up the phone.

I cried. I couldn't even get mad at her. I had created the whole situation. The monitor started beeping, so the nurse raced in and said, "Hey, you need to relax. You're upsetting the baby. What's going on with you? What are you stressed about? Breathe, honey. Come on, stop crying; it's not good, honey."

I didn't call anyone. I tried to relax. Then I remembered that I had left Camie's card on the counter in the kitchen. I wondered if Kim had found it yet. About an hour later, I got a text from Kim asking about the card that had Camie's name on it.

I texted back, "She stopped by and would like you to call her; she has been looking for you for years."

Then she texted back, "Cool, maybe I'll go out and have some fun like you do!"

I texted back, "Okay, if that will make you happy!" Then, the monitor really started beeping on the machine!

The nurse ran back in and said, "You really need to calm down."

She called the doctor in. The doctor did some checking and said, "The baby is in distress."

The nurse said, "We need to call one of your family members. Can you give us a number?"

I didn't want to give them Kim's number, and April was in New York. My mom was nowhere to be found, so I gave them Michelle's number and told them she was my sister. After speaking to Michelle, the nurse put me on the phone with her.

Michelle said, "What's going on, Carrie?"

"My stomach started hurting. I called the doctor and he told me to come in. They immediately admitted me, so here I am. Kim keeps calling me and yelling at me. She won't let me say anything; I can't even tell her where I am. She assumed I'm out with a boy and hung up on me. Then she texted me that she found Camie's card on the counter, so I told her she stopped by looking for her. Kim said she was going out and have some fun with her, and now the baby is in distress." I said all of this while crying.

Michelle said, "I'm going to call her."

"No, don't call her! Let her do her thing. That's our problem; we're not letting her live her life. I'll be fine, I just need to relax."

Michelle said, "We're coming up. We should be there in three hours, but you should know I'm going to call Kim. She would kill me if I didn't tell her."

"Michelle, can't you come and see that I'm going to be fine before you do that, so you can see that you don't need to call Kim?"

She said, "Okay, I'll wait until I get there, but no matter what, I need to tell Kim or her mother."

I said, "I tell you what. I'll call April when you get here to let her know they're monitoring me and that way she won't stress."

I lay in bed. I finally had to turn my phone off because I kept getting texts from Kim saying things like, "Is he fucking you good? Yeah, I knew you wanted that dick! Don't forget to let him hit it from behind." It was stressing me out more; tears were running down my face. How could she say those things? But I knew why, because I did go out and do those things while I was with her.

About three hours later, I was calm when Michelle and Vanessa walked into my hospital room. They both hugged me and said, "So how's everything going now?"

I said, "They're better. I've calmed down."

Michelle said, "Good, but we were calling you. Why did you turn your phone off?"

"Kim keeps texting me some not-so-nice things and it was stressing me out, so I turned my phone off."

Michelle said, "Okay, well, I want to talk to either the doctor or the nurse about what's going on."

I said, "Okay, I'll call them." I pushed the button and the nurse came in. When the nurse came in I said, "This is my sister and she wants to know what's going on with me."

The nurse assured Michelle I was going to be fine, as long as I took it easy and didn't stress out. Michelle said, "Okay, now you're either going to call April or you're going to call Kim. Pick one, Carrie."

I said, "Okay, I'll call April."

When I turned my phone back on, I had at least a dozen voice mails and a bunch of texts. I checked my voice mail and it was Kim, over and over, calling me names and yelling at me through the phone. I deleted them.

Michelle heard them and said, "She is really tripping."

Then we read all the texts. One said, "You're nothing but a whore! Why did I ever get with you?" Then another said, "I know what you're doing, and I hope he's going to marry you, because I don't want you anymore." Then there was another one that said, "Two can play this game," and one that said, "I just fucked Camie and it was good, so you don't have to worry about me. I have what I want now."

Before we could finish reading them all, Michelle took my phone and said, "Call April right now!"

But I was crying, and I needed to calm down. When I calmed down, I took a deep breath and called April.

She answered, "Hi, sweetheart."

I said, "Hi, are you busy?"

She said, "No, I'm having dinner."

I said, "Okay, I don't want you to get upset; everything is fine. I wanted you to know they admitted me into the hospital and they're monitoring me."

April asked, "Where is Kim? Why didn't she call me?"

I said, "She's here with me. I told Kim I wanted to call you myself."

She said, "Let me talk to her."

"She's out talking to the doctor; you know how she worries even though they keep telling her I'm fine. She keeps asking a lot of questions."

She said, "Okay, how long are they keeping you there?"

"I'll go home in a couple of days. Kim is staying here with me."

"Okay, as long as I know you're fine, but I hate that I'm not there. Maybe I should come home."

"No, they said that I just need bed rest, so what are you going to do? Watch me sleep? You'll be home soon enough."

She said, "Okay, but you or Kim better call me if something happens. Promise me."

"I promise."

She said, "Okay, I love you and I'll call you soon."

"I love you too and don't worry."

When I hung up the phone, Michelle asked, "Why did you lie to her and tell her Kim was here?"

"Because you know she would have jumped on the first plane out here and started having a fit if she knew what Kim was doing. She would not be very happy with Kim, and I don't want to come between Kim and her mother."

Michelle said, "Look, Carrie, I'm going to go find Kim and talk to her. Vanessa, can you stay here with Carrie?"

Vanessa said, "Of course, babe."

I said, "Michelle, no, let Kim go be happy, please!"

Michelle said, "Carrie, does she sound happy to you?"

"Yes, she said she was happy and that she has what she wants now. I mean, C.J. is the love of her life!"

Then Michelle started to say something, but Vanessa cut her off and said, "Babe, I got this! You listen to me, Carrie. I know for a fact, you are the love of her life. I watched that girl go crazy over you. I have sat up nights with her while she cried over you. All she wants is the way it used to be, before all of this big mess happened. She even wants to raise the baby as her own, but she's still dealing with the hurt you caused her. Look, Carrie, you created this, so you need to stop stressing and have some patience. I don't care what you say, I don't care what she says, she's in love with you and she wants you!"

I said, "So that's why she is out fucking this girl C.J.?"

Vanessa said, "To be honest, I don't think she is. I think she is trying to hurt you as much as you hurt her. And if she did fuck this girl, it's because she's hurting, which you should understand. So let's keep you calm and Michelle will deal with Kim, okay?"

I said, "Okay, Vanessa."

Then Michelle said, "Well said, babe!" She kissed Vanessa and then headed out to find Kim.

Vanessa came over to the bed and said, "I'm sorry, but it had to be said."

I said, "It's okay now. I understand a little bit more." We talked for a while and I ate the hospital food they brought me.

Vanessa was down in the cafeteria when Michelle came back without Kim. She said, "I wasn't able to find her anywhere and she isn't answering her phone, but I did leave a message on the door at the house saying that she needed to call me ASAP! I must have left her a million messages on her phone, so when she gets around to listening to them, she'll call me back."

I said, "She's really pissed at me! I should have let her sleep with me that night and none of this would have happened."

Michelle said, "Carrie, this was going to happen no matter what. It's stuff she has been holding inside of her. This is why she goes to counseling. She needs that, and I'm thinking maybe you two should go to counseling together."

"Yeah, that's an idea, but I don't know if she would want me to go with her. Can I ask you something, Michelle?"

She said, "Sure."

"Do you think she's with Camie?"

Michelle said, "To be honest, I don't know, but let's not think about that right now. We'll just try to get you well so that we can get you home."

"Yeah, but you know that's all I'm going to be thinking about."

Michelle said, "Well, I'm going to try and make you think about other things, like have you picked a name for the baby?"

"No, I'm letting April pick the name. I love making her happy."

Since I was staying in the hospital, I gave Michelle the keys to the house so they could stay there while they were in town. But they ended up staying in a hotel close to the hospital. I really couldn't sleep that night; no surprise there. I kept thinking about Kim in bed with Camie. What if she fell in love with her all over again? I told myself I needed to think about my baby and not stress out. I was also thinking about how I was going to tell April I needed to move out when she got back. It would not be good living there while Kim was with Camie.

In the morning, the nurse came in and said, "Good morning, honey. I'm going to help you take a shower." She helped me out of the bed, took me into the bathroom, then turned the water on and helped me into the shower. I was pretty big for someone a little more than six months pregnant.

After my shower, they brought my breakfast in. I really wasn't hungry. A few minutes later, Michelle and Vanessa walked in. Michelle said, "Good morning, how are you feeling?"

I said, "I feel good. I took a shower and they brought me breakfast. I really didn't like it."

Vanessa said, "Well, that's okay, because we brought you some real food."

I couldn't help myself. I had to ask, "Did you hear from Kim yet?"

Michelle said, "No, not yet, but I expect to any minute."

"So, she didn't come home last night? She must be sleeping with Camie. I guess she's going to be with her now, so I need to move out. There is no way I can see Kim with someone else."

Michelle said, "We don't know if Kim went home last night, remember? We stayed at a hotel, but Kim isn't going to be with her. I know Kim loves you too much. I want you to stay calm and we'll work this out, okay, Carrie?"

I agreed and said, "Okay."

Michelle said, "Okay, so, you're going to eat everything we brought you, because I know the baby is hungry." That was just like Michelle to change the subject very quickly. Then Michelle's phone rang and I looked at her as if to say, *Is that Kim?*

She said, "I have to take this call, it's my job." I started making small talk with Vanessa. "So have you started planning your wedding?"

She said, "Not really, we have a lot going on."

"I'm sorry, Vanessa. I know you guys have been taking on a lot with Kim and me."

Vanessa said, "Listen, that's okay; that's what friends are for. I'm pretty sure you'll be there for me when Michelle starts to get on my nerves. You know, she can be a big baby at times." We both started laughing.

I said, "Well, I really appreciate you two being here for me and the baby."

Vanessa said, "It's not a problem."

"You know what, Vanessa? I really love you guys and I'm so glad you two found each other." Vanessa said, "Well, if I recall correctly, we didn't find each other; you and Kim hooked us up."

"Yes, but you must admit, it was meant to be."

Vanessa said, "Yes, you're right, and I couldn't be any happier if I tried."

When Michelle walked back in the room, Vanessa walked up to her and said, "Is everything okay?"

Michelle said, "Yes, babe, they wanted to know how much time I needed off."

Vanessa said, "Have I told you lately how much I love you?"

Michelle said, "Yes, you tell me every day, and I love you more."

I said, "Aw, aren't you two sweet together. Michelle, when are you going to make an honest woman of her?"

She said, "If I had it my way, I would do it today. But she wants to have a big wedding, and here in California, it's not legal yet, thanks to Proposition 8. So we're going to Vermont to make it legal, after the wedding."

The doctor came in and asked if Michelle and Vanessa could step out while he checked on me. After he did, he said "You're doing a lot better. If you can promise me you're not going to stress out, I see no reason you shouldn't go home today. I'm putting you on bed rest, though, and you need to understand, this is serious. If you don't take care of yourself, you could lose the baby, or your own life."

I agreed to take care of myself and told the doctor I would, because I wanted to get out of there. I promised him. When Michelle came back in, I told them I could go home, and they were happy. Michelle helped me out of bed, and I started getting dressed. I still had to wait until the nurse came in to release me. While we were waiting, I asked if we could stop for ice cream on the way home. Michelle said, "You never told me how you got to the hospital."

I said, "Oh, I drove myself and it took me forever to get out of the car."

Michelle said, "So your car is here?"

I said, "Yes."

Michelle said, "Okay, I'll drive it home. You and Vanessa can stop for ice cream."

I said, "No, I want all of us to go!"

Michelle said, "Okay, we'll stop together for ice cream on the way home."

We stopped at my favorite place to get ice cream, the Sherman Oaks Galleria. I loved to get ice cream there; they always gave you those large cones with lots of ice cream. We walked through the galleria after getting our ice cream and then Michelle realized something. She said, "You're supposed to be on bed rest. Let's get you home."

I said, "Oh, okay, Miss Pushy," then we laughed. We headed home and when we got there, Michelle's note on the door was gone. I guess Kim had been there and just didn't call. Michelle took my stuff upstairs, and then Vanessa and I headed to the kitchen where we could see out into the backyard. Vanessa wasn't paying any attention, but I looked out at the pool and saw Kim making out with Camie. She had her pinned up against the poolside in the water. You talk about heartbreak! I dropped my ice cream and started crying.

Vanessa said, "What's wrong?" just as she saw what I was looking at. Then she called Michelle's name. Music was playing out back, so they didn't hear us or see us, but Michelle came running down when she heard the way Vanessa was yelling her name. When Michelle saw me crying, Vanessa said, "Look, Michelle; look at Kim."

Michelle said, "Take Carrie upstairs."

But I wouldn't go. I went out to the pool and said, "I'm glad you have what you want now!"

Then Kim yelled back, "Yeah, just like you! Is your boyfriend here? We can have a pool party!"

Michelle said, "Vanessa, take her upstairs now!" But I still wouldn't go. Michelle said, "Kim, stop it! Get out of the pool. I need to talk to you!"

Kim said, "Michelle, there is nothing to talk about. She does her own thing and I'm doing mine!"

Michelle said, "Kim, get out of the pool, now!"

Kim said, "No, I'm having fun and I don't care if she's crying; now she knows how it feels."

Camie was watching the whole thing. I guess she didn't care, because she had her girl back. Kim started kissing Camie some more, while I was having a nervous breakdown watching them. But I wasn't going upstairs. I said, "That's it, I'm moving out! I can't do this anymore."

Kim said, "Yeah, why don't you go back to your boyfriend's house!"

Then Michelle yelled, "Stop it, Kim!"

Kim said, "Stop what? She's been out fucking every Tom, Dick, and Harry, and you want me to stop?"

Michelle said, "Kim, you don't know what you're talking about."

Kim said, "Oh yeah, ask her where she's been for the last two days. She's been out fucking her boyfriend."

Michelle said, "Kim, stop it." Michelle was getting pissed now and said, "Get your ass out of the pool—now, Kim!"

But Kim yelled back, "Fuck you, Michelle! I don't have to do shit but stay in this pool! Look what I got; she's hot right? Oh, and Michelle, this one doesn't like dick, so I won't have the same problem I had with that one."

Her words were hurting me so bad, I fell to my knees crying, saying, "I can't do this anymore."

Michelle tried to help me, but I was too hurt to move. My heart was so heavy and it wouldn't let me get up. Then Michelle said, "That's it, Kim! Get your ass out now; I'm not playing with you! She has not been out fucking anyone. She's been in the hospital for the last few days. She lied to your mother by telling her that you were there with her, because she didn't want to come between you and your mother. I've been calling and I left you a note! If you would have called me back, you would have known this! Now get your ass out of the pool and tell your company good-bye!"

Then Vanessa started yelling, "Oh, my God! She's bleeding!"

Michelle shouted, "Call 911!"

Kim jumped out of the pool and said, "What have I done? Oh, my God! Carrie, baby. Let's get her to the couch, Michelle! Help me!" They got me to the couch and Kim kept saying, "Don't pass out, stay with me; look at me, Carrie! Baby, I'm so sorry. I love you, please forgive me, please!"

Michelle ran and got a cold towel to put on my head. Vanessa told Camie it would be best if she left. Then Camie asked Kim, "Who is this?"

Kim yelled at her, crying, "This is my heart!"

Camie said, "Wow, I can't compete with that," and she left.

I put my arms around Kim and said, "I love you. Can't you see that? I don't want anyone but you, baby. I'm sorry for everything. What am I supposed to do? You won't come back to me."

Kim was crying too and said, "I love you, too."

I said, "Kim, this isn't good for us. I need to go away. I can't be around you if I'm not with you; I'm killing my baby. I just got out of the hospital for stress today and now I'm bleeding over stress. I have to leave, I'm sorry. Everything is my fault, Kim. I did all this, so I should be the one who has to fix it, and the only way to do that is to go away."

Kim said, "No, baby, I love you. I don't want you to go away; I need you. Please don't leave me. I didn't have sex with her. I'll be with you, I promise."

I said, "Kim, you don't trust me, and look where your lack of trust has gotten us. I know it's my fault."

The paramedics came in and put me on a gurney. Kim started crying and said, "Michelle, what have I done?"

Vanessa was crying too, because she was so hurt by what had happened between us. Kim rode in the ambulance with me and tried to calm me down, while Vanessa and Michelle followed us in their car. On the way to the hospital, Kim was making all kinds of promises to me. "Babe, we're going to go away, just me, you and our baby. I'm going to take good care of us." Tears were running down her face. "I'm going to love you so much that you won't ever want to leave me. We'll get a house and go back to our world. I promise, baby, I'll never stop loving you; all you have to do is hang on."

When I got there, my doctor came in and did all kinds of things to save the baby. They wouldn't let anyone in the room while they were working on me. I was in so much pain and losing a lot of blood. The doctor said they were going to have to take the baby out, to save her. When they took the baby out, they took her somewhere, but I didn't know if she was going to be okay.

The monitor started going off and Kim ran into the room and said, "Baby, hold on."

The doctor said, "Get her out of here!"

And the last thing I said was, "But she's my wife."

* * *

Carrie died on September 17th at 7:21 p.m. that night. Kim hit her knees crying and screaming, "Why? Look what I did!" Michelle came in and tried to help Kim, but she was heartbroken just watching everything that was going on. Michelle got on the phone and called April to let her know what had happened. She could hear Kim in the background crying and saying, "I killed my wife! What have I done?"

April got there in the middle of the night. When April walked into the room, Kim was clinging to Carrie's body. She was still crying when she said, "Mommy, I killed my wife." April tried to calm her down, but there was no use.

The doctor came in and said, "I understand you're her mother. We did everything we could do to save her, but she lost too much blood. I'm very sorry." Although the doctor said Carrie died from loss of blood, I felt she really died of heartbreak. April sat and held Kim for about two hours while she cried. She knew she was going to have to admit Kim into the hospital. After that, April went looking for the nurse that was dealing with the baby. The nurse took April in to see her grandchild.

The nurse said, "Do you have a name for her?"

April said, "Yes, she's my little Angel." She weighed five pounds and three ounces when April took her home.

Part two coming in 2014

About the Author

From humble beginnings as a PA on a show, Kristy Cato knows exactly what hard work and dedication will get you as she was later promoted to Field Coordinator on an award-winning television show. Unfortunately, due to economic hardship and the recession, budget cuts would end Kristy's job. Every day Kristy would wake up, make her coffee and then sit down in front of her computer in search of a new job. "Day after Day" this became her routine and to no avail. As time went by, the process was most frustrating and she became very discouraged. This stirred unwanted emotions that she tried to tuck away through her work. It was one morning that she turned on her computer in search for that new job she so desperately wanted and needed, she somehow opened her word program and began to write. "It was crazy, how this story just poured out of me" says Kristy. Although, "The Dance My First Love" is "Fiction" everyone knows there is some truth to most stories. As she wrote, emotion poured out of her. Taking her back to when she was a little girl, until the memories of the heartbreak of her first love became fresh. She dedicated The Dance: My First Love to her first love. Although, her first love may never read it or even know about it. Kristy Cato says "It was amazing facing my fears and pain after all of these years." As most of us know, there is nothing like your first true love. Miss Cato encourages

those who have never experienced that first true love to embrace it when

it happens and not take it for granted. Kristy Cato resides in California

where she was born and raised…..

Made in the USA
San Bernardino, CA
26 December 2015